POUND

HARD HIT 10

CHARITY PARKERSON

COPYRIGHT PAGE

coincidental. All items contained within this novel are products of the author's imagination.

INTRODUCTION

Von lives by three relationship rules—no lies, no games, and no strings. Justin has him breaking all three.

Von knew the first time he kissed Justin that the man was different. Justin didn't play by Von's usual rules. He also knew Justin was way too passionate to be tied down by someone who travels as much Von has to with his team. For a while, Von was content with being Justin's part-time lover. That is, until Justin decides to be his no-time lover.

At first, Justin was star struck by the sexy hockey player. Von's brilliant mind, good looks, and delicious accent had Justin enthralled. He might have chosen to stay Von's friend with benefits forever if Von hadn't flaunted another man in his face. Justin might like Von, but he's no one's fool. Unfortunately, when he chooses to give Von one last chance, the man rips out his heart, leaving Justin broken and infuriated.

When Von ignores Justin's fury and refuses to go away, Justin is left with two choices. Either he can listen to Von beat on his front door for the rest of his days or he can let him in and pound some sense into the man who's ruined Justin for all others.

1

---

*J*ustin couldn't stop staring at the total on the cash register. It wasn't that he found the numbers especially fascinating. He equally wasn't concerned with over-spending on his groceries. It was the name flashing on the face of his ringing cell phone he was trying to ignore. The woman behind Justin in line had cleared her throat twice already and given him countless annoyed looks. He didn't care. There was nothing she could do or say that could possibly equal the destruction Von wreaked on his life.

After silencing his phone for the third time, Justin handed the cashier three twenties and a five, told her to keep the change, and headed for his car. With every step, Justin told himself a different lie. He didn't care to hear what Von had to say. Justin didn't want to see him. It didn't matter to him if Von was back in town. There was nothing left between them. A mousy-looking brown-haired woman walked past and flashed Justin a smile. Too late, he realized he hadn't smiled back. Every ounce of his concentration was locked on not feeling anything. That was what Von brought to Justin's life. He wasn't allowed to feel. After all, when he'd agreed to a one-night stand with the gorgeous German-born hockey player, Justin had sworn it wouldn't matter. Von traveled too much. They'd never see each other again, but they had—many times. Somehow, at some unnamed point, Justin had become the man's local piece of ass. It was a role Justin didn't want.

Justin drove the familiar route home, not seeing a thing in front of him and hoping he didn't kill anyone. All he could see was Von's gorgeous blue eyes and the way his dark blonde hair always fell across them. Justin's fingers itched with the need to push the man's hair out of his eyes. He wanted it with such an intensity it took Justin a moment to realize he was staring at the real thing. With his cut arms crossed over his massive chest, Von stood leaned against his F150 parked in Justin's driveway. His usual smiling lips were pressed into a hard line. Justin couldn't find the energy to open his car door. Von Wolf was larger than life. He was over six feet of smoldering good looks, talent, and fame. Justin was a nerd who should've never caught the man's eye. He was helpless against Von. Justin hated him a little for it.

Von opened Justin's door, as if Justin had been waiting for him to do so. "I've been calling."

Seeing nothing else for it, Justin climbed out. "Fifteen times, to be exact."

"So you've been ignoring me?"

Justin had to tilt his head back to meet Von's gaze. It wasn't fair for any one person to have so much of everything. "Seemed the fair thing to do, seeing as how I haven't heard from you in six months." Even as Justin made the claim, his hand went to Von's side. Hard abs were calling Justin's name, begging for his touch. It had been six long, excruciating months. Von would disappear again. He always did. Justin meant nothing to the man. The shittiest part was —Von didn't play games. He didn't mince words. Every single time, he let Justin know they were only temporary. They were no more than sex. His heart didn't care. It was deaf and blind. Too bad it wasn't also mute. His damn heart screamed in denial every fucking time Von walked away. Justin was the one who kept letting the man back in. He had no one to blame but himself.

Von's nostrils flared as he glowered down at Justin.

Justin fought the urge to punch Von in the stomach. The only thing stopping him was the sure knowledge the move would only hurt his fist.

"All you have to do is say you're finished."

Von's claim gave Justin the strength he needed to push the man away. He moved to the back of the car and popped the trunk. It was easier to speak his mind when he wasn't staring into blue eyes that had watched Justin as he'd orgasmed. "Fuck you for that, Von. You never say you're finished before moving on."

Von appeared at his side and grabbed all the bags of groceries in one swoop. "That's because I'm never done."

Justin turned away and headed for the door. He couldn't let Von see the way his words cut. A thousand retorts raced through Justin's mind. Unfortunately, the one that fell from his lips was the one that hurt the most. "That's funny. When I saw you on TV, openly dating that team owner, I would've sworn we were over."

Von didn't respond. Justin fought the urge to glance over his shoulder and check the man's reaction. It wasn't like there was anything Von could say anyhow. With his front door unlocked, Justin did his best to block the entryway. He couldn't let Von step inside. That was the point of no return —the point where Von always won.

He motioned toward the porch. "You can set those bags there."

"I can carry them inside," Von shot back.

Justin stiffened his spine and held Von's stare. "No."

Obviously realizing Justin wasn't joking, Von set the bags at his feet before meeting Justin's stare. "A couple of dates doesn't constitute dating. It was two dinners and a movie."

"Did you sleep together?"

"No." The way Von held his stare let Justin know it was the truth. Not that Von ever lied.

"Did you try?"

Von's expression never changed. "Yes."

Without a word, Justin grabbed the bags and tossed them inside, uncaring of the mess or if he destroyed anything. "You can leave now."

Instead of doing as Justin said, he continued holding Justin's stare. His blue eyes seemed different today somehow. Not colder, exactly. Justin couldn't decide what it was, but he knew he'd turn this moment over in his mind for weeks, trying to figure out what had changed. "You never said you wanted more," Von said, sounding near to accusing.

"You never said I wasn't enough," Justin shot back, surprising even himself. Normally, all Von had to do was show up, and Justin was his man. Not today. Not ever again. Justin's heart couldn't take Von's destruction any longer.

Von's gaze moved over Justin's face. A humming noise came from the back of the man's throat. The sound hardened Justin's dick, even as it stabbed him in the chest.

Because he wanted to ask Von what in the hell he meant by that noise, and his pride couldn't take asking, Justin did the only thing he could to save himself. He stepped backward into the house and shut the door in Von's face. A gasp tore from his lips as he released the knob. His shoulders heaved as if he'd run for miles. He'd done it. For the first time in his life, Justin had walked away from Von. Now all he had to do was figure out why the move left him filled with regret and disappointment.

VON STARED at the closed door and contemplated the merits of kicking it in. Most people would consider him a smart man. His IQ said he was a genius. Right now, he felt like a complete idiot. Worse, he was also a jackass who deserved to have Justin's door slammed in his face. None of that explained why he was smiling. That was all Justin's doing. This was why Von kept coming back. Justin was by far the most passionate person he'd ever met. That was why Von had never tried tying him down. Von's career kept him on the road. Someone like Justin needed constant affection. Von didn't want to be the reason the man sat around —starved.

Instead of giving in to temptation and kicking the door down, Von knocked.

"Go away."

A low chuckle escaped Von at Justin's immediate muffled words. The man didn't do a good job of hiding the fact he still stood on the other side of the door. While biting his bottom lip to keep from laughing, Von knocked again. The door flew open. Chestnut-colored eyes filled with rage stared out at him.

"What the fuck do you want?"

Von bit the inside of his cheek—hard. He knew laughing would only get him shut down, but goddamn. Justin looked hot as hell when he was angry. Of course, the man was sexy all the time. He wasn't a large man. In fact, he was compact

—like Von wanted to put him in his pocket. At five-five, Justin was near to being a foot shorter than him. His dark brown hair had more than a little curl to it. Von loved running his fingers through the soft locks.

"You slammed the door in my face."

"You deserved it," Justin shot back.

"I know."

The outrage bled from Justin's features at Von's answer, leaving Justin looking defeated. Von wanted the anger back. Otherwise, he was just the asshole who was hurting this amazing man. "Just one kiss, and I'll go," Von said, pleading his case.

Justin huffed. "You're like the dude who always claims he'll just put the tip in."

Von snorted. God help him. He couldn't contain it. "I'll do that too, if you'd like."

"I'm sure," Justin grumbled, but he took a step back, silently inviting Von inside.

Instead of falling on Justin and bending the man to his will, Von bent and picked up the groceries. He headed for the kitchen. Without glancing Justin's way, Von put the food away. It was ridiculous how well he knew Justin's home, as if it was his own. There was a box of artificial sweetener. Von shook his head as he opened the pantry. He set it on the shelf before pulling it back off again and shaking the box at Justin.

"This shit is really bad for you. It would be better if you used regular sugar, or better yet, honey."

Justin's gorgeous eyes flashed with irritation as he snagged the box from Von and tossed it on the shelf. "Why don't you mind your fucking business. Next, you'll start bitching about the candles I use releasing toxins in the air, or you'll tell me the toilet paper I buy causes ass cancer or some stupid bullshit like that."

"Now that you mention it," Von said, incapable of holding back his smart-ass tone.

Justin growled. It was hot. Damn, it had Justin's dick stirring. "Shut the fuck up, Von."

Von blinked. He'd never seen Justin like this before. "Wow, you're really mad, aren't you?"

"What clued you in?" Justin asked under his breath as he shoved the carton of milk in the fridge.

"You should drink Slim instead of Whole."

Justin's gaze slid his way. Von took a step back from the hatred flashing his way. "What?" A second too late, Von realized he should've stopped trying to tease Justin out of this mood long before now. It seemed insulting the man's milk was a step too far. "Did you just insinuate that I'm fat?"

Von swiped his hand over his face. "Okay. That's it," Von said. Without warning, he swept Justin off his feet and tossed the man over his shoulder. Justin tried fighting his way loose. Von easily held on to him. While turning in a circle, Von eyed the items that still needed to be put away. "Anything perishable left? Nope. Okay, then," Von said, talking more to himself than Justin as he headed for Justin's bedroom. "I tried playing nice, but you obviously don't want that."

"Put me down, Von."

"I thought maybe we could have dinner, and I could hold your hand. Hell, you never know, maybe we'd go to a movie. But no, you don't want that, I see."

"Put me the fuck down, Von."

When he reached the edge of Justin's bed, Von tossed him on top with enough force the man bounced. He dodged a knee to the groin as he covered Justin's body with his, pinning the man down with his weight. He'd never seen Justin look more outraged.

"If you don't get off me, you'll be sorry."

"I doubt it," Von said as he held Justin's jaw and claimed the man's mouth. Justin bit him—hard. Hard enough that Von tasted blood. He didn't let that deter him. If anything, Justin's rough treatment had Von's dick leaking. Damn, he'd missed the way this man rocked his world. Von bit him back. Justin moaned. Von damn near came in his jeans right then. Cool air brushed Von's back as Justin clawed his shirt off. He did mean clawed. Von was certain Justin took three layers of skin off his back along with the shirt.

"I won't enjoy it," Justin swore as Von peeled the man's jeans down his legs, setting his erection free.

Von could barely hear him past the blood rushing through his ears. "I'll do my best to disappoint you," he said before swallowing Justin's cock. Von's scalp stung from Justin pulling his hair. He didn't realize how much he'd missed the man beneath him until Justin's dick beat against the back of his throat. Von didn't mess around. He needed Justin a quivering mess. All Von had was a lubricated condom. There was little hope Justin would hang around while Von hunted down a bottle of lube. He needed the man relaxed and ready to go because Von intended to be inside him as soon as Justin's orgasm hit.

Justin's body tensed beneath him. Von hollowed out his cheeks even as he set his own erection free. When Justin came, Von transformed into the multitasking king. He dragged every last wave of satisfaction from Justin even as he suited up. Most days, Von could skate circles around everyone. Some days, he fell over while trying to pull on his pants. One thing he never did with anything less than grace was get inside Justin. As Justin's tight heat pulled him inside,

Von realized several things at once. He still had his shoes on. His pants were only halfway down his hips. The biggest realization of all, he was such a fucking idiot for trying to date anyone else. Justin clung to him. Their tongues fought for supremacy even as Von fell victim to Justin's perfection.

Von strained and moaned, seeking what only Justin gave him—some form of inner peace. After tearing his mouth away from Justin's, Von pressed his forehead to the man's shoulder, squeezed his eyes shut, and focused on release. Justin bit his shoulder, sinking his teeth into Von's flesh and setting him free. A roar tore from his throat as the pressure tightening his balls exploded into a blinding light. The air left his lungs. His spine bowed. Von forced his eyes open so he could stare down at the man who brought him so much pleasure. Justin looked... sad—like his moment was over, and now Von would be gone again.

"I'm sorry it's me," Von gasped against the man's mouth as he captured Justin's lips. He didn't know how else to explain the many thoughts rolling around inside his head at once. He was sorry he was the one Justin had fallen for. Von couldn't apologize enough for being the one who couldn't stay away. Most of all, he was just sorry.

2

*L*uka: *I'm in town on business. Can we meet for lunch?*
   Von: *Tell me a time and place. I'll be there.*

If Justin hadn't opened his eyes at just that moment, he would've never known. He would've gone on, happily forgiving Von without fully recognizing how deep the man's lack of care for Justin went. But he had. His eyes had opened and latched on to Von texting another man while leaning across him as if having not a care in the world. It wasn't just any other man either. Luka's name blared out at Justin from the face of Von's phone. Justin ground his back teeth, trying not to elbow Von in the ribs. The fucker was seriously making lunch plans with the same dude Justin had seen Von dating on the news. It was too much. Justin had endured too fucking much. His whole body ached from the bullshit.

"You need to leave."

Von's sexy eyes jumped from the phone to Justin's face. "I didn't mean to wake you."

Heat radiated from Justin's body, and not in a good way.

He snorted at Von's asinine observation. "That's obvious. Get out."

A deep line appeared between Von's eyes. "Are you okay? You don't sound so good."

Justin's throat burned—like he'd swallowed live fire ants. Still, it had nothing on the pain in his heart. "My throat hurts. It's probably from all the bullshit I've swallowed today. You need to leave."

Ignoring him, Von touched the back of his hand to Justin's forehead. "You're burning up. Do you have a thermometer around here?" Von climbed from the bed, giving Justin an unhindered view of bare skin. He hated the way his eyes took in every inch and lingered on parts they shouldn't. "I'll text Luka back and tell him lunch is off. You need me here."

"Are you fucking kidding me? Seriously. Are you shitting me right now?"

The rage—it was deep. His body was too weak to respond in the manner Von deserved—a swift kick in the ass. Justin's eyes burned. He couldn't tell if it was due to a raging fever or the knowledge he meant nothing to Von. Justin hadn't busted the man. It was obvious Von didn't care if Justin knew. His actions sent a clear message to Justin— he'd date who he pleased. Justin could accept it or end things. In his heart, he'd always known he meant nothing to Von, but Von had never been intentionally cruel before now. All Justin could do was stare at the ceiling and hurt.

"Here." That one word from Von was all the warning Justin got before a thermometer was shoved in his mouth. He dutifully shifted the cold device beneath his tongue as Von pressed the button, switching it on. Justin eyed the man's face with an odd sort of disconnect. Even knowing the man had broken him didn't detract from Von's good looks. He had a small but deep scar beside his left eye. His nose had been broken at some point. The man lived a rough and tumble life. He was strong and genius-level smart. On paper, Von was perfect for Justin. In reality, the man was a cruel bastard who made dates with other men while his nude body still pressed against Justin in Justin's bed. The thermometer beeped. The deep line between Von's eyes was back.

"Okay. Let's get you up. I'm taking you to the doctor."

"No." Damn, it hurt to talk. "Once you've made plans with someone else while still in my bed, I'm done. I should've never let you back in. Goddamn, I'm such a fucking idiot." The more Justin spoke, the more his throat burned and his heart broke. Seriously, it was like the same knives ripping at his throat also shredded the tattered remains of the stupid organ beating in his chest.

Von's frown deepened as he pulled Justin into a sitting position. "Luka is a married man."

Oooh, goddamn him. The German accent had thickened on Von's claim. Justin wanted to punch him in the dick. Unfortunately, he couldn't lift his arms. "That's a new low, even for you."

A puzzled expression crossed Von's features. "Luka is no more than a friend, and our lunch was business."

"A friend you tried to fuck," Justin shot back. Shit, his head spun.

"I'd planned to ask you to join us," Von said, sounding distracted as he moved to gather Justin's clothes. With clothes in hand, he returned to Justin's side and tossed a shirt over Justin's head. "If you'd like, you can tear me to shreds and give me the third degree after you're better. Right now, we need to get you dressed and in the car."

Since Justin was feeling worse by the second, he didn't

argue as Von dressed him as if he were a child. He did his best to help, but his body was like a leaden weight. Once they were both clothed, Von pulled him to his feet. The room spun. His stomach churned. "Jesus." The word came out in a whisper, sounding as if it floated in from a distance rather than falling from Justin's lips. Everything went black.

&

JUSTIN HAD BEEN in and out for hours. Despite the nonstop fever reducer and IV, his fever wasn't budging. Von had no fingernails left. He'd chewed them all down hours earlier. The odd thing about Justin's delirium was—it hadn't diluted his anger toward Von one iota. Von would worry over that later. Right now, they had bigger issues. So far, they'd tested Justin's white blood cell count, done a strep test, spinal tap, liver function, and thyroid function. No one would tell him a thing. He'd never been more ready to put his fist through a wall.

Von was so busy nursing his rage, it took him a moment to realize Justin's eyes were open again. The flush of his overheated skin made his eyes seem that much brighter.

"Why are you still here?"

Von winced at how scratchy Justin's voice sounded, as if it pained him to speak. The doctor said it was due to dehydration and not strep.

"I'm taking care of you."

A harsh snort reverberated off the walls of the tiny room. Justin's eyes fell closed. "I don't need you. I don't need anyone."

Von fought the urge to wince. He hated that Justin didn't need him. "I know, but I need to be here."

Justin growled but didn't open his eyes. "That's stupid.

You could easily leave here and never think of me again. God, I wish I'd never met you." Whoa. That hurt. "My whole life I've been less than everyone else, but never as much as I have been since meeting you."

Since Justin was the sexiest man he'd ever met, brilliant and passionate, Von had no idea what Justin was talking about. "How so?"

Justin's hands lifted before falling back to the bed. Von wasn't sure if Justin meant he had nothing, or he was too weak to talk with his hands. "Growing up, we lived in this small one-horse town about an hour south of Nashville. It was the worst place in the world for someone like me— small, nerdy, and gay."

Von already knew this, but he let Justin talk it out, especially since he didn't think Justin would remember any of this anyhow.

"We used to vacation here every summer. While we were here, no one ever judged me. The moment I graduated, there was no other option—to my mind— than Coastal Carolina. I was right. Once I was in college here, things got better. After getting my degree and landing an awesome job, I thought everything would be perfect."

Justin did have a kickass job. He was a Research Engineer for a Biopharmaceutics company. The man was amazing.

"I was wrong," Justin said, surprising Von. "Because I met you. I tripped over this gorgeous, gigantic, and famous hockey player in the middle of the grocery store."

Literally. Justin had turned the corner, tripped over Von's large feet, and nearly hit the floor. Von had caught him before it happened. Their eyes had met. Von had been a goner. Unfortunately, now, Justin wasn't finished tearing down that beautiful moment.

"I was so, *so* fucking stupid to think someone like you—who's always had people chanting their name—could ever truly want me. Such an idiot. I get it, though."

Von blinked. His chest burned. "You get what?" Von's voice came out sounding gravelly.

"I get why you're the one for me, and I'm nothing to you."

For a full minute, shock rendered Von speechless. He opened his mouth, intent on setting Justin straight, whether he remembered it or not. The door opened, cutting him off. Dr. Meyers strolled in.

"I had a thought," the man said without preamble. "Has Justin had any recent surgery?"

Von shook his head. "Not that I'm aware of."

"Yes," Justin said over the top of him.

Von's gaze shot toward the bed. He felt oddly betrayed he hadn't known that.

Dr. Meyers moved to the edge of the bed. He read Justin's vitals as he spoke. "Good. You're awake. Tell me about your surgery."

"Arthroscopy on my right knee."

The doctor immediately flipped the sheet back and inspected the knee. "Your leg is purple. Is it cramping?"

"Yes."

"I'm pretty sure you have a blood clot. That explains our inability to break the fever. It's an inflammation of the blood vessels. Are you having any chest pain or trouble breathing?"

"No."

The doctor nodded. Von was freaking the fuck out on the inside. Blood clots meant bad things. "Let's find it and then we'll talk."

"Okay," Justin said, sounding calm if not more than a little tired.

Von waited until the doctor left the room. "I'll call your parents."

Justin's gaze met his. "No. I'll call them when I get home. Otherwise, they'll drop everything and come here. Not only do I not want them hovering over me, they can't afford to make the trip. I'm used to being alone. This is no different."

Aggravation made Von's skin feel too tight. "You're not alone."

"If you say so," Justin said, closing his eyes again. "Don't let the door hit you in the ass on the way to your lunch date with someone else."

"Goddamn it," Von muttered under his breath. "Lunch was ten hours ago, and I haven't left your side, nor do I intend to. Go the fuck to sleep, Justin. I'll take care of you."

Justin didn't say anything else. Von eyed the man's pale face, wondering why his silence felt more like a "fuck you" than his words had.

❦

It took three days for Justin's brain to clear from the fog. Each of those three days were a blur. The only thing he knew for certain was Von never left his side. Some brown-haired guy had shown up with a bag of clothes for Von. He'd showered in Justin's hospital room. Ate every terrible meal alongside him. Shown care and worry over Justin that Justin had never expected. He only wished he could recall every second because Justin had no doubt he'd never see Von again once he was fully healed. If there was a god in Heaven, he would not. It was too hard. Hurt too much.

"Why are you still here?"

Von didn't look up from the book he read. It was a huge tome. No doubt it was also nonfiction. Sometimes Von could be downright boring in his tastes. *It was no wonder I caught his eye.* Justin bit back a groan at the thought. Von turned the page. His eyes moved over the contents.

"Why didn't you tell me you were having surgery? You know I would've dropped everything. I know you don't have anyone here to help you." Von continued staring at his book as he asked his questions.

Justin released a sigh. It sounded exhausted, even to his ears. "Why would I think you'd drop everything? Not only had I not heard from you in six months, you were also openly dating some guy. Not to mention, your team was in the playoffs. You couldn't drop everything."

Von finally looked up. His gaze moved over Justin's face, but his expression gave nothing away. "Then you should've waited to have your surgery until the playoffs ended." Von shook his head. "I suppose it doesn't matter now. At least I was there when you passed out. Otherwise, you might've died."

Justin's face screwed up in confusion. He felt it happen. "Are you waiting for me to thank you?"

Von turned another page, even though he hadn't looked away from Justin. "No. I'm waiting for you to apologize."

A pain bloomed behind Justin's eye. He rubbed his forehead. "Why am I apologizing?"

Von turned another page. "For not telling me about the surgery."

"Huh," Justin grunted.

"And scaring me," Von added.

"Wow."

"And for thinking I'd leave your bed to go on a date with someone else," Von continued, ignoring Justin's sarcasm.

"It's not as if I pulled the idea from thin air."

"Mostly for thinking we're over," Von said over the top of Justin, as if Justin hadn't spoken.

"No."

At his response, Von finally closed his book. "No, what?"

"No, I won't apologize," Justin said, surprised by how calm he sounded. Inside, he seethed. "You don't get to disappear from my life, date someone else, and then expect me to say I'm sorry."

Von stood and set his book aside. Still, his expression didn't change. The stirring in Justin's chest had him thankful they were no longer monitoring his heart. Von moved to stand over Justin, forcing Justin to tilt his head back to hold Von's stare. The man didn't stop coming. He flattened his palms on either side of Justin's head and leaned in until they were nose to nose. Justin was certain he hadn't blinked since Von closed his book. He was also glad they'd finally let him get up and brush his teeth. That random thought went further at proving how Justin always only thought of Von's comfort.

"Is my number still programmed in your phone?"

Justin licked his lips. With Von so close, he could practically taste him. "Yes."

"Then I didn't walk away from you. You chose to let me go. I'm always the one calling you, because you're a sickness for me. This last time I left, I decided I wouldn't call you again until you called me. Was it childish? Yes, but I obviously failed at my own test, and at least I can admit I didn't feel secure in whatever it is we have."

Von had him there. He did always call first. Justin's pride kept him from being the one who called—like he begged for the man's attention. "Kiss me." Goddamn it. That *was* his voice, whispering a plea for Von's touch. He might've called it back if an ounce of triumph had touched Von's features. Instead, the man's gaze turned heated.

"I'm already hard as a rock. If I kiss you, I might develop a limp."

Justin's fingers moved without thought. He needed to know if Von lied. Justin shaped the other man's erection through his jeans. A hum rose in the back of his throat. Von's eyes fell closed. Justin took advantage and captured Von's lips. For a second, neither of them moved. Then Justin's head hit the bed as Von pressed into him and ate at Justin's mouth. Their tongues clashed and teeth tugged at each other's lips. Justin could barely breathe beneath the onslaught. He didn't care. In truth, he'd always secretly expected Von would be the death of him somehow. A light knock landed on the door. Von jumped away and was reseated before Justin had his eyes completely open. His breath came in gasps. Dr. Meyers strolled in. Von stared down at his open book, but his gaze remained fixed upon one spot, as if seeing nothing.

"Are you ready to go home?"

Justin tried working up a smile for the doctor. "More than ready."

"Good. I'll get the paperwork together. Mr. Wolf has been briefed on what to watch out for, and what to do if you show signs of another clot. I have a feeling he'll take good care of you." Justin's gaze slid Von's way. The doctor kept talking, unaware of the weight crushing Justin. "Make sure you get your blood thinners filled before going home and take them as prescribed."

"I'll make sure he doesn't miss a single dose," Von said, interrupting.

Dr. Meyers chuckled. Justin couldn't look away from Von. "As I said, I think you have a fierce protector who'll watch over you better than we can." Justin couldn't hear a word past the roar in his ears. Von spoke as if he intended to come home with Justin—like Justin would never be alone again. The doctor shook Von's hand. Von nodded while the doctor's mouth moved. They both smiled as if they were old friends. No one noticed his panic. Justin couldn't tear his gaze away from Von. The moment they were alone again, Von came to his feet.

"Where was I before we were interrupted? Oh, yeah," he said as he moved to stand over Justin. "Right here," he said before capturing Justin's mouth. Sound rushed back to Justin's senses, overloading them. The reason for his choking terror was one he could never, ever share. The way Von acted with the doctor—the way he was treating Justin now—it was a trick. It had to be. There was no way what he'd seen in Von's eyes the moment he'd said he'd take care of Justin could be real. It had to be the lighting in the room or something related to his near-death experience. There was zero chance the love he'd seen in Von's gaze was real. No way at all.

3

*V*on barely stopped himself from chewing through his cheek. He could feel Justin's gaze boring a hole in the side of his head as he drove. Time was short. He needed to make his confession before they reached Justin's house, but—when it came to Justin—Von was weak.

"I have something I need to tell you."

"Okay." Justin sounded calm if not a little wary.

Von decided to jump in with both feet. "For the record, I did take your concerns to heart, but your parents are waiting at your house." Von rushed to explain while Justin was still gathering his strength for the storm. Von could feel it brewing. "I get that you didn't want them hovering while you were in the hospital. You were in no shape to be entertaining well-meaning people, but they're your parents. I also get they couldn't afford the trip. That's why I paid for them to come. I've been keeping them posted, and your mama has been cleaning your house until it shines, hoping you won't have to do anything for a few days." Von recognized he was rambling. He just couldn't seem to stop.

"Thank you."

"Your papa mowed your grass and even changed the oil in your car. I guess so he'd have something to do, hoping to be useful. I get that."

"You're amazing."

Von couldn't stop. "Please don't be mad. I just know if I had kids, I would want to know and be there if anything happened, even if they were grown."

"I'm not mad."

It finally sank in that Justin wasn't raging against him. He glanced Justin's way. "You're not?"

Justin's smile was sweet. It melted Von's heart. "No. There was no way I could've avoided telling them forever, and Mom would've been pissed and came even though she didn't have the money. I'll pay you back."

"Uh, no. You won't."

"It's like you want me to be mad," Justin said, reaching over and running his fingers through the back of Von's hair, belying his words.

Von softened his tone. "Look, baby. You know that money didn't make a blip in my bank account, and you also know I never do anything I don't want to do. Just let me have this, okay?"

Justin brushed his fingers through Von's hair again, making him want a nap. "Okay."

Von released his breath. He had no idea why Justin was being so agreeable, but he had no intention of digging and ruining things. "Do you need anything else before we get home?"

"No. It sounds stupid, since I've been doing nothing except sleeping for the past three days, but I really want a nap. I'm so tired."

"That's probably the meds. It'll take a while for you to

get used to them," Von said as he snagged Justin's hand and brought it to his mouth. He could feel Justin watching him. Without thought, Von's tongue shot out and stroked the inside of Justin's wrist. A small sound escaped Justin at the contact. Von went hard. Everything Justin did turned him on, as if the man owned the playbook on Von's body and knew exactly what to do, say, and what sounds to make to torture him.

Justin's driveway came into view. Von swallowed his growl of frustration. The man's parents were inside. Justin needed his family right now. Sometimes it was hard for Von to fight his nature. He wanted Justin alone—needed to ensure the man would be okay. For now, he would share Justin. Tomorrow, who knew? Maybe Von would finally confess everything.

Once inside, Von lingered on the fringes, watching as Kate fussed over Justin. When he'd called and offered to fly them out, she'd been understandably upset but not surprised Justin hadn't wanted her there. Justin had always been the type to worry over everyone else's comfort. He was also fiercely independent. No doubt, if Von hadn't been there, Justin would've found a way to handle things on his own. Although Von was glad he'd meddled and gotten Justin's parents on a plane, there was a small part of him that wished he could have Justin to himself. The man's anger seemed to be thawing, and Von didn't want to lose the headway they were making. Some things in life took precedence. Justin's parents getting to see him was one of those things.

"You didn't tell us you were dating a professional athlete," Jeff said, speaking up for the first time. "To be honest, ever since you came out, your mom's been hoping for a stylist. Something to do with eyebrows and threading. I don't know. I was only half listening, but a hockey player? That's awesome."

At Justin's horrified expression, Von bit the inside of his cheek to keep from laughing. Justin had warned him once about his parents. They were Justin's biggest cheerleaders. Unfortunately, they didn't know what they were cheering for half the time. They just wanted Justin to be happy. Since their goals were aligned with Von's, he wasn't offended in the least.

"Now, your sister, I'm expecting her to bring home a girl who drives a truck and calls us all 'dude' any day now."

"Jesus," Justin said under his breath.

Von swallowed back his laughter. Justin shot him a desperate look. Von wasn't going to make it. His face burned from the effort it took not to throw his head back in a huge guffaw. He straightened away from the wall. "I'm going to take a shower. A real one. The shower they had at the hospital was made for smaller men."

All eyes moved his way. Kate smiled. "Okay, sweetie. I washed the clothes from that overnight bag your friend left when he dropped us off from the airport. They're folded and on the bed. I didn't want to go snooping through the drawers to figure out which belonged to you."

Von flashed her a grateful smile. "Thank you. Justin hasn't given me a drawer... yet." Kate turned a disbelieving look Justin's way. He made a run for it before she unleashed her lecture.

As he waited for the water to heat up, Von chuckled while he stripped. It wasn't fair of him to make Justin's parents believe his relationship with Justin was more than it was, but it kind of was more than Justin gave them credit for being. Maybe neither of them had admitted to deeper feelings, but they were there. If he didn't feel anything for

Justin, he wouldn't be so pissed off all the time because Justin never called or texted. Von was always the one to make first contact. The first move. The first everything. Feeling insecure was a new thing for Von. But damn, Justin brought it out in him. Every time he thought about Justin, Von calculated the odds of them making it, and the numbers weren't good. Von traveled six months out of the year, but fuck. He traveled six months out of the year and he'd never met anyone like Justin. The man was one of a kind.

Hot water streamed down Von's body. Closing his eyes, he tilted his chin up. The memory of the first time they kissed flared to life in Von's mind. Justin had been telling him a story about a teacher who'd marked him absent every day despite saying hi to him each morning when Justin entered his class. Justin had laughed. There'd been a certain light to the man Von couldn't resist. Before he could stop himself, Von snagged the man by the back of the neck, pulled him close, and pressed his lips to Justin's. Justin had been so surprised, instead of kissing Von back, he'd burst into laughter. It hadn't been a small chuckle. The man had thrown his head back and roared with laughter, making it impossible for Von to kiss him. Not that Von had stopped trying. Nor had the man's laughter ruined the moment. Instead, Justin's laughter had been like a punch to the chest, stopping Von's heart and sending adrenaline pumping through him. He wanted to keep him.

Fingers slipped down Von's spine. A smile tugged at Von's lips. His dick stood at attention at the unexpected move. "Your parents are here."

Justin's lips touched his shoulder. "I told them I needed some sleep."

"You're such a rebel." Von's words came out sounding more breathless than he intended.

"It wasn't a complete lie," Justin said. His lips moved lower down Von's back at the claim. "I fully intend to go to bed soon. First, I need to do this." Justin sat on the edge of the bathtub. Von slapped his hands against the wall, hanging on for dear life as Justin toyed with his asshole. He widened his stance, giving Justin all the access he needed to Von's body. Even though Von wasn't one to bottom, Justin knew how to make his body sing. He'd learned to let the man have his way, because Justin would make it worthwhile.

Justin rolled Von's balls between his fingers before fisting Von's cock. He waited until he had Von panting before slipping one finger in Von's ass and twisting. Von's knees weakened. He locked them to stay upright.

"You're always sexy, but when you're submissive, you're beautiful."

Von heard the words as if they came from a tunnel. All he knew was his body's needs. "You're supposed to be resting." Von had no fucking clue why he was arguing. He craved the release Justin's hands promised. Above all else, he needed Justin to be okay.

"Hey, I'm sitting." Justin's voice was filled with laughter.

Von pressed his forehead to the shower wall. He couldn't argue with Justin's logic.

"You're being awful lazy," Justin said, pressing against something internal and dragging a moan from Von. "It's not like you to not take your pleasure."

"I'm exhausted after sleeping on that cot," Von said, rather than confessing how much he savored Justin's touch. He'd almost lost him. Ten minutes after the doctor decided Justin had a clot in his leg, it had broken loose and almost stolen Justin's life. Von had never been more scared. Justin was fine, and Von never wanted to let go. His man was touching him. It felt a lot like heaven.

Justin's palm slid down Von's erection. "I've got you."

Von gasped as sparks of pleasure pulsed through him. "You always have."

Justin's motions stilled. "Have I?"

The sad note to Justin's question had Von's heart turning over in his chest. He sprang into action, pulling Justin to his feet and dragging him beneath the stream of water. His body screamed he was an idiot for pulling away while on the edge. Some things were more important. Without a word, Von shampooed Justin's hair, gently massaging his scalp. He washed all the suds away before starting on soaping up the man's body. Von took great care to ensure he got every inch of Justin's body clean, leaving the man panting. He could tell Justin a thousand times he was important. Special. Von wanted to show him. Justin's erection tapped Von's cock. Their gazes met and held. A wave of emotion washed over Von. He opened his mouth and almost ruined his life by confessing everything.

❦

A LUMP LIVED in Justin's throat, choking him. The way Von stared at Justin made him thankful the man held him upright. Von's lips parted. Justin broke. After going up onto his toes, he captured Von's mouth. They grappled for control. He already knew Von would win. Not only was Justin weak from being ill, Von was twice his size. That last detail never stopped Justin from making Von work for it. Using his size against Justin, Von easily forced his will upon Justin. The kiss turned sweet—lips barely brushing. Justin's eyes burned. Sometimes, Von's actions fooled Justin, making him discontented with their arrangement. Every now and then, Von tricked Justin into feeling loved. It was a cruel thing to be held by Von—stroked and babied. When the man left again, and he would leave, Justin would fall back into the same depression he always did. Reality would crash down on his head, leaving him broken. He simply had no idea how to go from being with Von to anyone else. No one could fill the man's gigantic shoes.

"Let's get you dried off and into bed."

Justin stood still, biting back a smile as Von swiped a towel down their bodies. He knew Von was turned on and had been close to orgasm before pulling away earlier. Justin also knew Von was trying to take care of him while ignoring his own body's needs. As much as Justin appreciated the sentiment, Von was about to have the tables turned against him. Justin let Von lead him back inside the bedroom as if he would willingly go to bed. Von stumbled to a stop as the bed came into view. Justin bit his lip to keep from laughing. The sheets, blankets, comforters, and even the pillows were gone. Nothing more than a bare mattress awaited them.

"What the hell? I walked right by here on the way to the shower and the bed was made. Where did everything go?"

Justin shrugged. It was hard as hell to hang on to his innocent expression, but this was too important to fuck up. "Guess they disappeared." While shaking his head, Justin released a heavy sigh. "I suppose this means you'll have to go to bed with me. With these new blood thinners, I'll freeze without something keeping me warm."

Von glanced over. A small snort escaped Justin at the man's expression. He'd never seen anyone look more put upon. "You hid the blankets from your own bed? That's... I don't even know."

Justin blinked, trying hard to fight back his laughter.

"Why would I steal my own blankets?" Justin let the towel he wore fall to the floor, leaving him nude. "You better get to warming me up. Otherwise, I might catch my death."

Von turned. Justin had to force himself not to take a step back. A deadly light entered Von's eyes as he closed the distance between them. "You're such a fucking tease." Von growled the words as he grabbed Justin by the ass and hauled him against Von's massive frame.

A wicked smile pulled at the corners of Justin's mouth. It was out of his control. "Nope. If you recall, I was more than willing to please you in the shower, but you chose to stop things."

Von tilted his chin to the ceiling as if realizing how right Justin was. "Fuck. I forgot how bad your bed squeaks."

Justin reached for Von's hand and linked fingers before pulling him toward the bench at the foot of the bed. Bare-assed, Justin sat and stared up at Von. Von's chin hit his chest. Hunger filled the other man's gaze. Justin smirked. He knew what seeing him at perfect dick-sucking level was doing to Von. No doubt the man was already picturing Justin taking him between his lips. Since that was exactly his plan, Justin didn't hesitate to lick Von from root to tip while holding the man's stare. The man's eyes glazed over and a flush touched his cheeks. Justin gave himself a mental pat on the back before opening his mouth and taking Von to the back of his throat.

Von pulled Justin's hair, taking what he wanted. Justin's balls grew heavy, reminding him that his own erection wanted attention too. While hollowing out his cheeks and sucking, Justin reached between his legs and fisted his cock. Saliva ran down his fingers as he pumped Von's dick at the same pace. His eyes were heavy with the need to shut out the world and focus on the pleasure. Justin couldn't stop staring at Von. In the shower, Justin hadn't lied. When Von gave in and let Justin have control, he was the most beautiful man Justin had ever set eyes upon. Knowing he owned Von in that moment had Justin's lust skyrocketing.

He kept a steady pace, allowing Von's dick to scrape the roof of his mouth before sucking him down his throat and repeating the process. Justin knew he could toy with Von's crown and balls, dragging out the man's torture. This wasn't about making Von last. Justin wanted to see him explode. He needed to feel the hot jets of cum shooting across his tongue. The pressure beating at Justin's crown made him wonder if he would come first. He knew he could stop at any time and ensure Von got off before him, but everything felt too good. Von's hands ran over every inch of Justin's skin the man could reach. Justin didn't want that part to ever end. There was nothing better than Von's hands on his body.

Every muscle in Justin's body tensed, anticipating release. He stroked faster, needing relief, even as he sucked hard on Von's dick. A sharp gasp escaped Von, sounding loud in the otherwise silent room. Hot cum hit the back of Justin's throat, nearly making him choke, since he hadn't been focusing. He jerked back, swallowing, hoping to catch his breath. Von's cum hit him in the face at the same time as his own orgasm hit. Justin didn't have time to recover. Von's mouth slammed down on his. The man's tongue filled his mouth, stroking and retreating as Justin rode out the waves.

Von kissed a path to Justin's ear. Their harsh breaths filled the air. "We need another shower."

A low chuckle was the only response Justin could dredge up in the aftermath of Von.

❧

HE WAS TIRED, but he wasn't. Since he'd spent the last three days sleeping, Justin's mind raced all over the place with unspent energy while his body cried foul. Watching Von sleep seemed like a better pastime than resting. When Von smiled, he looked nice and radiated friendliness. The rest of the time, Von looked hard—like a male version of resting bitch face. He looked unapproachable in those moments. It was funny he didn't soften in his sleep. It was his bone structure. At a skeletal level, Von was hard. He also ground his teeth in his sleep. Justin smiled at the muscle jumping in the man's jaw.

With an inner sigh, Justin slipped from the bed, moving slowly as not to wake Von. Once he was certain Von wouldn't stir, Justin moved to the closet and retrieved the blankets he'd stuffed inside earlier. After covering Von, Justin found some clean clothes and quietly dressed while keeping one eye locked on Von's sleeping form. With his body sufficiently covered, Justin sneaked from the room, leaving the man in peace.

Justin found his mom on the couch, watching daytime TV with the volume turned so low there was no way she could hear it.

"Where's Dad?"

Kate didn't startle. It was obvious the eyes she'd grown in the back of her head the moment she'd become a mother were still in good working order. "He grabbed a cab and went out. You know being trapped in the house isn't his thing. Knowing him, he's probably found a sports bar somewhere and is currently bragging about his son who snagged a pro hockey player."

Without thought, Justin rolled his eyes. It seemed that being around his parents caused Justin to revert to teenage responses. "There's a lot more to Von than playing hockey."

"I know, but that's all your dad needed to know about the man to give his approval. Is he still sleeping?" Kate asked as she stood, gesturing for Justin to take the couch.

He dutifully sat, letting her baby him by grabbing him a throw blanket and tucking him in. "Yeah. All they have at the hospital are those horrible chairs that pull out to form a bed two feet too short for someone Von's size. I'm sure he never slept more than ten minutes at a time for the past three days."

"He's a good man," Kate said, claiming the loveseat.

Justin nodded. "He is." Justin's words came out sounding more thoughtful than agreeing.

"Then why haven't you given the boy a drawer?"

Justin fought the urge to rub the spot in his chest that ached at her question. "Mom, he doesn't want a drawer."

"Yes, he does," Von said, appearing at Justin's side. He urged Justin over, claiming half the blanket and snuggling in close.

Justin stared at Von—shocked. "You do?"

Von smirked. It was hot. "Of course. I told you the other day I've been waiting for you to tell me you wanted more."

Justin was certain Von had not said that, but with his mom sitting there, hanging on every word, Justin was in no position to argue. Instead, he stared at Von's profile and blinked back the sting of tears as hope flared to life inside him. They weren't supposed to be this couple. Justin wondered if Von was putting on a show because his parents were there. Once they left, no doubt Von would return to normal, and Justin would be crushed. Not that he would ever let Von know it.

"I'm starved. Is anyone else hungry?" Von asked, as if he hadn't turned Justin's world on its head.

Kate stood. "What would you like? I'll fix you something."

Von waved away her offer. "Please, sit. One of my team-mates, his wife owns a restaurant that serves only clean foods. She also delivers. I'm thinking, since Justin only keeps junk food around, we should give her a call."

Justin huffed. It was only his mom's presence keeping Justin from telling Von where he could stick his clean diet.

"I'm always telling him he should eat better, but I'm his mom. He'll never listen to me."

Something in Justin's jaw popped as he swallowed down all the words rising in his throat.

"*Ja*. Exactly."

Justin couldn't take it. He had to argue about something before he burst a blood vessel. "Did you just '*Ja*' my mother?"

Von shook his head. His eyes took on a thoughtful edge as if he was running through the conversation in his mind. "Sorry. Yes. I've lived here for over twenty years, but some-times—when I'm not thinking—I forget to speak English."

"Don't apologize," Kate said, sounding scandalized Justin had made him feel the need to say he was sorry. "Eng-lish isn't your first language. I'm amazed at how fluent you are."

"That's because he's a genius," Justin said, fighting a sudden wave of exhaustion.

A tinkling laugh sounded from his mom. "So now you want to flatter him after scolding him."

Justin closed his eyes and leaned his head back. "I'm not flattering him. Von really is a genius. He has an IQ of like 180 or some shit."

Kate blew out a whistle. "Really? That's amazing. Yet you

chose to play sports for a living?" Kate asked, sounding more like the mother Justin knew.

Justin felt Von shrug. "180 is a bit generous, but there's a science to winning. It fascinates me." Von's claim sounded as if it came from a distance, even though the man sat pressed against him. He was so warm. Justin couldn't get close enough to Von. Von shifted next to him, pulling Justin against his chest and wrapping one gigantic arm around him. No matter how hard Justin tried to open his eyes and rejoin the conversation, he couldn't lift his eyelids. They were too heavy. Von fell into an explanation of how he'd moved to the US with his father when he was barely a teenager. Justin listened to the words rumble against his ears until sleep carried him away.

4

"Carolina Chuggers' forward, Von Wolf, is this year's hottest unrestricted free agent, going into the—" Von switched off the TV as he walked by, cutting off the report.

"Hey, I was watching that," Justin argued. "They were talking about you."

Von scoffed. "I know. It's the same story every year."

Justin had no idea what that meant, but he was willing to let it slide. "You have your shoes on. Are you leaving?"

After moving to his side, Von pulled him to his feet. "We're leaving. You've stopped jogging since your surgery, and I know how much you love it, so we're going together."

Justin blew out a raspberry. It had been three weeks since his stay in the hospital, and even longer since his surgery. Von hadn't left his side the entire time for longer than it took for him to run home and get more clothes. Justin knew it was time to get back into his exercise routine. "But you're in so much better shape than I am. It's not fair to make me start back with you witnessing my limitations."

Von's incredulous expression almost made Justin laugh

—almost, but there was still the issue of running. No one laughed when facing an hour of jogging. "What do you mean by that?"

"I'm just a little guy," Justin said, biting back a laugh. He knew—any second—Von would realize he was teasing and make him pay.

"You're just a little..." Von's expression turned baffled. He paced across the room and Justin stole the opportunity to sit back down. Von glanced his way. "What are you talking about?"

Justin mimicked walking with his fingers. "You're tall. I'm short. If I have to start back with you, it'll kill me."

Von rolled his eyes. "This sounds like an excuse to be a lazy ass to me."

A smile that felt evil, even to him, pulled at Justin's lips. "Nope. I just think I should start smaller. You know, with something where height doesn't matter, but I'm still okay-ish at doing it."

Von braced his hands on his hips. His eyes lit as if he was beginning to catch on. "Such as?"

Justin pretended to think it over. "Well, they say sex burns a lot of calories."

"A hundred calories in an average session, and I say you blow okay-ish out of the water. There's nothing the least bit okay-ish about having sex with you."

Justin wasn't surprised Von knew the exact numbers. "There's nothing average about us, baby. I'd say a hundred calories is nowhere near our numbers."

"We should buy a calorie counter and find out."

Von was always all about the facts. Justin just wanted to fuck. "Later."

Justin drew a slow breath through his nose as Von crossed the room. His spine relaxed into the couch. He felt stalked. "I expect you to do all the work. You're the one who needs to get back into your workout routine."

Dropping his gaze to Von's feet, Justin slowly inspected every inch of the man's body. By the time he was staring at Von's sexy blue eyes, Justin's dick beat a pattern against the inside of his shorts and each breath came harder than the last. Von's body was perfect in every way. It was like he'd been pulled from Justin's dreams and carved from marble. Justin bit his bottom lip—anticipating.

"You are such a sexy man," Von said, his accent thickening.

He felt sexy with Von staring at him like he'd be the man's next meal. "I was just thinking the same thing about you."

"How about this? If you run a quick half mile, I'll spend the rest of the day doing whatever you want." Von raked Justin's body with his heated stare, letting Justin know the man meant his boast. He would do anything.

Justin stood and faked a yawn. "Nah. I think I'll go back to bed instead." He made it halfway to the bedroom before Von overcame him. Justin hid a wicked smile as Von's arms encircled his waist from behind, before pulling Justin back against a solid wall of chest.

"We were still talking."

Justin shrugged. "You didn't sound like you want to play with me, so I'll go play with myself."

Without warning, Von shoved his hand beneath the waistband of Justin's workout shorts. He palmed Justin's already hard cock as he opened his mouth over the cords of Justin's neck. His eyes fell closed at the sensation of Von's strong tongue stroking his skin. Justin moved against Von's hand. The dude wasn't playing around. Von's rough hand encircled Justin's throat, forcing his head back against Von's shoulder. He pressed his lips to Justin's ear and spoke against its shell.

"Is this what you want? Do you want me to fuck you, suck you, and turn you over my knee?"

Justin whimpered as images of Von doing just that flared to life in his mind.

Von increased his pace, obviously determined to make Justin come. "Would you like for me to bend you over the bed, shove my face between your ass cheeks, and tongue your hole until you beg?"

Justin writhed in Von's arms. "Please?"

Von bit his lobe. "First, I'll jerk you off and make you feel good. Then, you'll get your fucking running shoes on and meet my demands so I can spend the rest of the day inside you."

That was it. Von had won this round. Justin was too close to orgasm to argue or put up a fight. No way in hell was he walking away from the release Von offered.

"Von."

Von's grip tightened on Justin's neck, forcing him to turn his head for Von to capture his mouth. Justin moaned even as he stroked Von's tongue with his. They explored each other's mouths. Tongues seeking and retreating. Exchanging bites and harsh breaths. Each tug of his cock brought Justin a little closer to the edge. A burst of electricity surged through his body, drawing his balls up in anticipation of release. He struggled toward the promise of ecstasy. Every muscle in his body tensed. It was right there, teasing him. Explosion hit, rocking Justin to his core. Von's mouth, covering his, muffled the screams. Justin shamelessly rocked against Von's palm, riding out each pulsation.

Justin's heart turned cartwheels inside his chest. It was moments like these—when his guard was down—Justin's mind became the enemy. He was in love with Von—had been for a long time. If he'd felt nothing for the man, it wouldn't have bothered him in the least when Von disappeared on him. This time, his situation was worse than ever before. Von was there, pretending he felt the same. When he left, and he would, this would be the time Justin was done for good. He cared too much. Von's touch always lit him from the inside. The way his mind worked fascinated the hell out of Justin. They felt like partners in every endeavor. It wasn't fair for him to be alone in this.

Von's kiss turned sweet. Justin ate it up, taking what he could. It didn't matter he was covered in cum and his clothes stuck to his skin. Von was still stroking him softly and kissing him like he didn't want it to end. With one final nip of Justin's bottom lip, Von pulled away. His cheeks were flushed and his eyes looked unfocused. For a moment, he stared at Justin with such hunger, Justin couldn't breathe.

"To hell with it," Von said, sweeping Justin off his feet. "I don't care if you ever run again," Von added as he headed for the bedroom.

Justin stared at Von's hard features as the man gently set him on the bed, and he did something he'd never done before. He prayed. Justin prayed if anyone was listening, they'd let him keep this man. Not once had Justin ever asked for anything. Everything he had he'd earned through sacrifice and hard work. Von was the one thing he didn't know how to win without help. Maybe Von would never love him. That was okay because Justin loved him enough for the both of them.

❧

VON SPENT his days working out and dealing with business

issues while Justin worked. It was almost time for a new season. He had to be ready—for more things than one. Every day, when Justin came through the door of what Von was quickly beginning to think of as their house, Von couldn't control the happiness that exploded in his chest. Today was no different. As Justin came through the door— expensive suit draping his gorgeous body and hair ruffled as if he'd been running his fingers through it—Von had to stop himself from flying to his feet and meeting the man halfway. Instead, he held still. He let his hunger grow as Justin crossed the room and came to stand over him.

"Hey sexy," Justin said, sounding tired. "How was your day?"

Von couldn't take another second. He snagged Justin's waist and pulled him into his lap. Their lips met. Von's heart stopped. Air filled his lungs as if he hadn't enjoyed a real breath all day without Justin. "I've been waiting to do this," Von answered against Justin's lips.

For a moment, Justin melted into his touch and kissed Von back every bit as furiously, before pushing away. His serious expression had a hint of worry sneaking in. "Is it okay if I ask you something?"

The hint of worry increased tenfold. "Always."

Justin winced as if he expected his words were about to sound idiotic. "What are you about?"

Von's mind blanked. "What?"

The discomfort written on Justin's face increased. "I mean, I'm thrilled you're here and I don't want it to stop, but what's changed?"

Although he was certain he knew what Justin was getting at, he didn't know what the man needed to hear. "Nothing."

Justin's face fell. "Oh." He tried pushing his way from Von's lap. "What do you want for dinner?"

Von held tight, refusing to let Justin get away. "I think you misunderstand." Von was the one wincing now. "I've always had strong feelings for you." He blew out a sigh. No doubt he sounded like a fool. "But I didn't want you tied down by me, because I'm gone a lot. Jesus," Von breathed, hearing how badly this was going and incapable of stopping now. "Before just recently, you never gave me the impression you wanted more."

The way Justin eyed him, as if Von was fucking this up, wasn't helping matters. "Uh-huh. Go on."

"I really want that empty drawer in your bedroom," Von said before he could change his mind. Justin smiled. Von's gut twisted. He could feel the moment slipping away. The one where he could be completely honest. Von wasn't used to being scared of losing anyone. "That's not true." The words spilled out in a rush, stealing Justin's smile. "I mean, it is, but it isn't."

"Okay," Justin said, dragging the word out and proving how badly Von was confusing the situation. "What is the truth?"

Fuck. Had someone turned on the heat? Sweat broke out across his forehead. He was scared to look at his hands. If he did, he might learn they really were shaking. "Well, if you think about it—in all reality—we've been dating two years. I mean, if you don't factor in the whole I never said we were dating thing."

"You're not making things better," Justin said, confirming Von's fear that he was indeed making this worse by the moment.

"I want all of you—" Von's phone rang, cutting him off.

He scrambled to answer. Anything was better than continuing down this road to hell. Anything at all. "Hello?"

"Hey, man. What's up? It's Jamie."

"Jamie..."

Jamie huffed. "Roussel."

Surprise rendered Von mute for half a second. "Hey. It's been a while. I didn't know you still had my number." He really hadn't. Von had met Jamie and his husband, Hawke, through Luka. They'd chatted for a while, and Von genuinely liked them, but he hadn't believed Jamie would ever speak to him again. After all, Jamie was famous. Everyone wanted to be the man's friend. Von wasn't special.

Justin eyed him curiously. Von winked at him.

"Of course. I never lose anything. Anyhow, Hawke and I will be cruising through the Carolinas this weekend. I have a few concerts lined up that way, and we were wondering if you'd like to do something while we're in town?"

"I'd have to check with my man."

"You should bring him along. You know I'm great fun. What's his name?"

"Justin." Justin was smiling again. Some of the tightness in Von's chest eased.

"Awesome," Jamie said, sounding genuinely excited at the prospect of meeting Von's man. "Tell him how much fun I am and bring him along. How about Saturday night?"

Jamie was a hard man to resist. "Okay. I'll text you the address."

"Cool. See you then."

"Okay. See you." Von disconnected the call. "It seems I have friends coming in town this weekend and they want us to go do something. Is that all right with you?"

The way Justin's eyes shone with happiness had Von mesmerized. "You called me your man."

Von shook his head. He couldn't believe how blind Justin could be. "You are. That's what I've been trying to say." He took a breath, determined to do this right. "Do you remember our first date?"

Justin nodded. "We got pizza."

A luminous smile pulled at Von's lips, making his cheeks ache. "You were wearing a blue button-down shirt and khakis, because you'd just gotten off work. We chose a booth, and you sat in the center of the bench, obviously expecting me to sit across from you."

Justin snorted. "But you didn't. You bullied your way into my side of the booth, pushing me over and crowding my space with your big-ass body."

"Yet you still tried getting away," Von added. He could still remember every detail of that night. "Your elbow and knee barely brushed mine. I kept scooting closer, trying to get you to touch me. Then you did."

Justin chuckled. It was a low and sexy sound. It drove Von to continue.

"One second, you were trying to get away. The next, your hand slid up my thigh, stopping just short of where I wanted you. That is, until I met your gaze."

"You should've seen your face," Justin said with a snort. "Priceless. That place was low lit and private. Not to mention, the tablecloth did a good job of hiding the way I stroked your cock beneath the table."

"Jesus," Von breathed, going hard. He'd never forget that night. He'd been forced to order their food and act as if nothing happened. All the while, Justin had jacked him under the table with the lightest of touch. They'd been left with no other choice than to steal the cloth napkin he'd been given to hide the fact he'd come all over it.

"I wonder whatever happened to that place," Justin said, sounding nostalgic. "We never went back."

"That's because I've failed you a lot over the past two years, but I knew it even then."

A baffled expression crossed Justin's features. "Knew what?"

"That given half a chance, I would fall in love with you."

Justin's lips parted in surprise. Von wanted to kiss them. He craved their plump texture between his teeth. He needed to feel Justin's moans against his mouth. "Have you been given half a chance?"

Von held Justin's stare. He needed this man to know every word he spoke was the truth. "I think we both know I've been given a hundred chances, but I get what you're asking, and yes. You don't realize it, but every time I leave here, I'm paralyzed with fear that you'll meet someone else. Someone who'll give you the life I haven't. No one else will ever love you half as much as I do."

Justin didn't react right away. His hesitation damn near had Von hyperventilating. "Will you think less of me if I say I'm completely terrified right now?"

"No, why?" Von asked, taken aback by Justin's question.

Justin answered while holding Von's gaze and slowly drawing him closer. "Because I've never loved anyone before you, and I'm realizing how much power you have to break me. It'll leave me in pieces if you decide you don't want this."

"I fucking want this," Von said, claiming Justin's mouth before the man could say anything else to stab him in the heart. Even just the idea of Justin being left heartbroken made Von's chest hurt. He wasn't toying with this man. Von was in deep. He knew Justin didn't see things the same as him, but all the times he'd walked away was because he loved Justin. Von didn't want him sitting around, hurting because Von couldn't be there. He'd seen hockey wives. Those marriages went one of two ways—either they were there for only the money and didn't care if their man cheated with anything moving, or they ended up shattered by a career that stole every free moment from family. A thousand times he'd wondered why any of the players bothered. That is, until he met Justin. Now he understood how one person could steal another's soul. All it had taken was one night, and Justin had robbed him of everything.

5

*F*or the tenth time, Von caught Justin fidgeting. He set his hands over Justin's, stopping the motion. "If you don't want to go to dinner with my friends, I can call them and make up something."

Justin flashed him a smile. "I'm good. Plus, it's almost time for them to be here. You can't call them now."

"It's never too late for me to make you happy," Von said, never meaning anything more in his life. "I know you don't like meeting new people." He did too, which made him wonder now why he was putting Justin through this. Yeah, he wanted Justin to meet his friends. It was like offering another slice of himself to the man who owned him, but he didn't need this. He should call Jamie and tell him not to bother.

Justin shut him down before he could dig his phone out. "No. I want to meet your friends."

Von's gaze moved over Justin's face, searching. "Are you sure?"

Before Justin had time to answer, a rapid beat landed on

the door. "Told you it was too late," Justin said, heading for the door.

Von was right on his heels. "Nope. I don't mind slamming the door in their faces."

Justin looked scandalized as he met Von's stare. "You will not." He yanked open the door and kept a tight hold on it as if daring Von to try as he greeted their guests. "Hey."

Jamie and Hawke Roussel stood, wearing complete opposite expressions on the other side. Hawke's light-brown hair ruffled in the wind and his smile warmed the outdoors by ten degrees. Jamie eyed the bushes nearby as if he expected someone to jump out at them. Still, he was the first to react to Justin's greeting. His blue eyes swung their way. Dimples appeared, and he shook his head, forcing his choppy brown hair out of his eyes.

"Dude, is this really your house?" Jamie asked as he strolled inside, arm slung over Hawke's shoulders and uninvited. "I swear every rich person I know is deciding to stay humble—except for yours truly, of course."

"Actually, this is my house," Justin said before Von could set Jamie straight.

"Oh," Jamie said, brightening. "See, that makes sense. You look like the humble sort. Von, on the other hand, is too extreme."

"Part of me feels like I should be insulted," Justin said, sounding the opposite as he bit back laughter. "The rest of me is dying to know who you are."

Von stifled a snort as Jamie's mouth fell open. He slapped his free hand against his chest. "You, sir, are dead to me."

Hawke rolled his eyes even as he gave Jamie a consoling pat. "I'm Hawke," Hawke said, stepping out of Jamie's hold and extending a hand to Justin. "This is my husband, Jamie. He's not really an idiot and you're not really dead to him."

Justin accepted Hawke's handshake. "Justin."

Von caught himself eyeing Justin's every reaction to Hawke. Everyone undressed Hawke with their eyes and stared at him in longing. If the man's unique green eyes didn't stop a person cold in the street, the man's beautiful heart left them enthralled. Jamie might be the famous one, but Hawke always stole the show. Yet, somehow, Justin easily moved his gaze from Hawke to Jamie, as if he didn't see what everyone else saw.

"Why am I dead to you?"

Jamie moved closer, eyeing Justin from head to toe. He seemed willing to give Justin a second chance. "Do you listen to grunge rock?"

"No. It makes my ears bleed."

Jamie released the most dramatic gasp Von had ever heard. "You're dead to me times two." He grabbed Hawke's arm. "Hold me back, baby," he said, pretending to strain against the arm he held against his chest.

"I'm not for everyone," Justin said, dismissing Jamie's antics.

Jamie dropped Hawke's arm and shrugged as if nothing happened. "Oh, well. I guess we won't have to worry about you fawning over me all night, then."

Justin glanced Von's way, as if seeking answers. Von decided to put the man out of his misery. After flanking Justin's side, Von tucked the man beneath his arm. "Jamie is one of the biggest names in grunge rock. We'll probably be dining tonight while surrounded by a security team and listening to people scream his name."

Jamie huffed. "You weren't supposed to tell him, Von.

When people don't know who I am, they're so much easier to fuck with."

"No one fucks with Justin but me," Von said, sounding way more possessive than he intended.

Rather than being put off, Jamie's smile grew. "Yay. Jealous men rule," Jamie said, doing a little fist pump.

"This is the oddest conversation I've ever had," Justin said under his breath, looking lost.

Hawke glanced around the room as if looking for a place to sit. "He's had too much sugar today," Hawke said, heading for the nearest chair.

"Nu-uh," Jamie argued, tossing a wink Von's way while Hawke wasn't looking. Von got it. Half the time, Jamie's outrageous behavior was for Hawke's sake. He loved making his husband smile. He followed on Hawke's heels. "You know Easter candy is my favorite, and I hoard that shit. If you hadn't threatened to throw it out, I wouldn't have been forced to eat all of it in one sitting."

"Easter was over three months ago, baby," Hawke said, sounding ridiculously patient. "Half that stuff was probably out of date, and we don't have a ton of room on the tour bus."

"Chocolate doesn't go bad," Jamie said, stamping after Hawke and hovering over him with his hands on his hips.

"Actually, it does," Von chimed in, not really taking sides. He just couldn't help himself.

"It does?" Jamie asked over his shoulder.

"Don't ask Von," Justin said, leading Von toward the couch. "If it was up to him, all sugar would be banished from the planet. If you put your candy in the freezer, it'll last longer."

"That's not..." Von waved his arms wildly, reduced to speechless mimicking in his frustration. He wasn't sure why he was arguing. Maybe it was the way Justin always dismissed his thoughts on a healthy diet. "I didn't say anything about banishing sugar."

Jamie sat down at Justin's other side, ignoring Von. "Shut. Up. You can freeze candy?"

Justin shrugged. "Of course. At Halloween, they make these peanut butter candies dipped in white chocolate. You can't buy them any other time of year. I always buy a ton of them and freeze them. I think Von threw them out while I was in the hospital."

Two sets of hostile eyes turned in Von's direction. Hawke was the only one who looked amused by the discussion.

"You threw out the man's candy stash? Not cool, dude. How would you feel if he threw out your steroid stash?" Jamie leaned across Justin and poked Von's bicep, as if emphasizing his point.

Von swiped his hand over his face. "Jesus. I'm not on... I didn't... for fuck's sake," Von said, throwing his hands in the air, before focusing on Justin. "I never left your side when you were in the hospital. If anyone threw out your candy, it was your mama. I might be opinionated, but I'm not stupid."

"Why were you in the hospital?" Hawke asked in an obvious attempt at calling the conversation under control.

"Blood clot issue," Justin answered, sounding every bit as calm. It struck Von. The two men had somehow reduced Jamie and Von to baseless arguing without once losing their cool. The thought brought a smile to Von's face. Jamie and Hawke were the perfect couple. They were everything Von strove to be with Justin. Jamie traveled all over the world and had people of all sexes, colors, and ages throwing themselves his way, but the man never strayed. Hawke loved the goofball, no matter how outrageous he became. If Justin had the same effect on him as

Hawke had on Jamie, it meant he was right. Justin was the one.

&.

JUSTIN STARED at Von's slightly baffled expression and bit back a laugh. He was so in love with this gigantic know-it-all. Since he'd obviously confused the hell out of Von, Justin decided the man had enough teasing for the night.

"By the way, Jamie," Justin said, snagging the man's attention away from attempting to feel up his husband on the sly. "I was only messing with you earlier. I know who you are. Hawke called a few days ago to double check the address since the one Von gave you didn't match the one in your address book. We talked for a couple of hours. He thought it would be funny if you met someone who didn't know you for once. So... can I get a picture with you?" Justin bit his lip after asking the question. He felt a bit idiotic, but no way was he missing a shot at getting a photo with the great Jamie Roussel.

Jamie shot Hawke a sly look. "You're so bad." Hawke blushed. "It's hot," Jamie added, bringing an unexpected flush to Justin's cheeks as well. With those two words, Justin knew in his heart the pair had an amazing sex life. Before Justin had a chance to recover, Jamie slid closer. "Get out your phone. You're my new best friend, because you like candy and me."

By the time Jamie finished taking pictures in as many ridiculous poses as possible, Justin's stomach hurt from laughing. Justin turned toward Von, determined to show off his new pics to Von. Before he could say a word, Von kissed him. It didn't matter they weren't alone, or that Jamie flanked his other side. Von didn't hold back. Justin couldn't explain why Von's actions affected him so deeply. Maybe it was pride. Von wasn't ashamed, even with his friends sitting there. Justin tried pulling away. Von held tighter and deepened their kiss.

"I guess we should head out."

At Jamie's suggestion, heat scorched Justin's cheeks. He pushed at Von's chest. "We have people watching us."

"No worries over here," Hawke said, his voice heavy with laughter.

"Nope," Jamie said, adding his two cents. "I'm only butting in because I have a security team waiting outside. But just wait until we get in the car. I love the back of a hired vehicle. It's something to do with the lighting." Indeed, Jamie did sound nostalgic. "I could do some naughty shit to my Hawke in the back of a hired car. In fact, I asked him to marry me in the backseat of a hired vehicle. It was awesome. He said yes and everything."

"Obviously," Hawke said. The tiny smile hovering on his lips didn't match his sarcastic tone. It took every ounce of Justin's willpower not to sigh. They were in love. It was beautiful.

❧

THE RESTAURANT JAMIE chose was peaceful, and more than happy to clear out a private room so they could eat in peace. They'd come in through the back and no one had spotted them. There were no screaming fans or otherwise. Once they'd settled in, Jamie had settled into his normal more subdued personality. Somehow Von had ended up with Jamie at his side instead of Justin, but he didn't complain. Justin sat across from him and they'd played footsie under the table. A hundred different times, Von caught himself smiling over the ridiculousness of it. They were the miracle he'd never expected to find.

"Are you moving to Phoenix with Von?"

Von was in the middle of telling Jamie how he could make a homemade plasma cutter— because apparently, Jamie had a real interest—when Hawke's question floated down the table. Von stopped mid-sentence. Everything inside him froze. He sought Justin's gaze. The man's face had gone pale.

"We haven't discussed it." Justin's words sounded hollow. Von couldn't even blink. He should've anticipated this— asked Jamie and Hawke to stay quiet.

To Von's horror, Jamie latched on to the conversation. "Oh, yeah. I forgot Phoenix snagged you for forty-two mil and six years. That's a sweet deal. Has your house sold yet?"

A smile that felt brittle even to him stretched Von's lips. "Yeah. A month ago." His mind scrambled for a way out of this conversation. He needed to make it stop. Justin's dead eyes said it was too late. Pandora's box had already opened, and he couldn't shove the topic back inside.

Hawke smiled, obviously oblivious to the pain in Justin's face. "Have you found a new place in Phoenix?"

Von shook his head. Justin looked away and stared at something to his left.

"Well, I'm sure some of your new teammates will know the right neighborhoods and whatnot."

"I'm sure," Von said, pushing the words past numb lips.

Justin glanced over, his smile brittle. "I hate to cut this short, but I have a long day ahead of me tomorrow. This has been amazing. I've truly enjoyed meeting both of you."

"Same here," Jamie said, motioning for the check. "I have a few concerts out this way. Maybe we can get together again before we head for the west coast."

"I would love that." Even though Justin's words sounded genuine, his eyes were still flat.

Justin's subdued silence on the ride home had Von more frightened than he'd ever been in his life. He couldn't lose Justin. That was why he hadn't said anything. He'd been certain he could find a way to keep Justin and this new position if only he had enough time to think on the situation. Now, his time was up.

Most people wouldn't have noticed Justin's silence, especially in light of Jamie's upbeat chatter filling the car. Von couldn't concentrate on anything else. He reached for Justin's hand, half-expecting rejection. The tightness in his chest eased a hair when Justin linked fingers with him. Von ran through several speeches, discarding each. Nothing he thought to say did justice to the feelings in his heart. He always over-thought things. That was why he was awesome at all things scholarly and sucked at dealing with people. He'd never gone to school. His father had educated him, and with Von's ability to absorb details, he'd finished by twelve. Unfortunately, that home education had given him little interaction with children his age. Hockey didn't count. Where he was from, training wasn't a child learning sportsmanship. It was more akin to being prepped for war.

He didn't need anyone psychoanalyzing him to know he'd missed key lessons on life. Everything he'd been taught at his father's knee hadn't covered friends, falling in love, or considering others. He brought Justin's hand to his mouth and kissed the tip of each finger. It wasn't that he hadn't considered Justin when taking that Phoenix contract. It was more that he'd seen it as a blessing he could share with the man he loved.

Even after they said their goodbyes to Jamie and Hawke, and made their way inside, Justin didn't speak. Von wished the man would rage. He couldn't fight a reaction he couldn't see. Justin did a damn good job of hiding his emotions.

Von was the first to break. "Say something."

Justin worked his belt loose and threw it on the couch without meeting Von's gaze. "There's nothing I can say. It's a done deal."

At odds with every reaction Von expected to have, his temper hit the roof. "Don't you care? Does this mean nothing to you?" Von asked, motioning between them.

Rather than matching his rage, Justin's shoulders fell. He met Von's gaze and every ounce of anger fled. Justin hurt. That had never been Von's intent. "You mean everything to me," Justin said, his words not much louder than a whisper. "But I recognize when I'm beaten. I can't compete with your world. You were just a dream for me."

"Is that what you think?" Von asked, pushing the question past his rapidly swelling throat. Justin didn't respond. Von closed the distance between them. "Do you think I'll just pack my stuff and walk away like we never happened? All the times I've told you how much I love you, was it just words to you?"

"Your job—your very demanding job—is now in Phoenix. Tell me how that's not packing your things and walking away?" Justin didn't sound angry, merely defeated.

"Because you're coming with me," Von said without having to think it over. As the words left his mouth, all the anger, pain, and worry slipped away. In truth, Von had always known this was the only way. Not only that, but this was why he'd waited so long. He didn't want to give Justin time to think. Von wanted the man by his side— forever.

Justin blinked. "What?"

Von nodded. His voice gained strength. "Forty-two million, Justin. You never have to work again. Hell, if you're interested, you can travel with me part time. See the world. We don't have to be apart."

"What?" Justin repeated.

His arms encircled Justin's waist. He towed Justin closer, their bodies molding. There was hope in Justin's gaze. "I want you with me, baby. Quit your job. Sell this house. Come live with me. I don't want to be apart."

"Um."

Von kissed Justin before he could turn him down. "Keep me," Von begged as he changed angles. He sucked Justin's bottom lip as he worked the man's T-shirt higher. "Please, Justin? I don't want to lose you," he begged as he moved to Justin's jaw and worked the shirt over Justin's head. He tossed the shirt aside before reclaiming Justin's mouth. His heart couldn't take hearing Justin tell him no. Now that his offer was out there, desperation filled him. Justin had to come to Phoenix with him.

"Don't think. Just say yes," Von said as he worked the button loose on Justin's jeans. He dropped to knees. "I'm officially begging," he added, setting Justin's erection free.

Justin's fingers ran through his hair, massaging Von's scalp. There was so much love in Justin's gaze, Von couldn't look away. "Yes." Von's eyes fell closed as Justin handed him the world. The weight of the world lifted from his shoulders, leaving him feeling lighter than he had in ages. He kissed Justin's crown. A low gasp reached his ears. His tongue shot out, tracing the man's slit before circling the tip. They had forever. The realization had Von moving tortuously slow. Flipping his gaze upward, he held Justin's stare as he opened his mouth and allowed Justin's cock to slip inside.

"I love you. You're not going anywhere without me." Justin's harsh-sounding confession broke Von. He took

Justin to the back of his throat, determined he'd never let Justin regret this night.

§

TERROR CHOKED Justin as he stared down the line of his body at the man at his feet. He'd been through every emotion tonight. Justin had lost the world and gained twice as much in the span of an hour. His head spun from the ride. That was what being with Von was like. It was the highest of highs and the lowest of lows while hitting everything in between. Justin had just agreed to give up everything to be on that ride forever. He couldn't wait to get started. He wanted to hide in the bedroom.

Von licked his cock while undressing him, stealing every fear. A lump formed in Justin's throat as he watched Von's massive shoulders roll with every move the man made. Those shoulders now belonged to Justin in a way they never had before. They'd start a new life in a new town where everyone would know they were together. It was almost as good as getting married. Jesus. This was really happening.

Justin's head spun. His body's needs drowned out his worries. Von never gave him time to think. He always bullied his way in. No one could stand against this. Von's tongue caressed every inch of Justin's dick as he swallowed Justin's cock. The man's throat squeezing him felt too good. He struggled for air as Von hollowed out his cheeks. The man's mouth was so hot and wet. Von's fingers dug into Justin's ass, squeezing and massaging as his head bobbed, allowing Justin's dick to saw in and out of his willing mouth. All Justin could do was hold on to Von's shoulders, lock his knees, and let the pressure build. His nerve endings danced with anticipation. Every muscle in Justin's body drew up tight, bracing for explosion. A half second before Justin blew, Von pulled away and shoved Justin to the floor. He spread Justin's knees wide, spit on his asshole, and speared him with his cock while finishing Justin off with his hand. Cum coated Justin's stomach. His greedy ass tried milking an orgasm from Von as his inner muscles pulled the man deeper. Justin's body burned and sang. He'd never felt fuller or more complete. The sight of Von fucking him was the sexiest vision he'd ever enjoyed. The man's muscles strained and were hard with lust. He kept hitting something internal, causing tiny aftershocks to ripple through Justin. Justin stared into the face of unapologetic ecstasy as Von came. He whispered Justin's name. Tears pricked the backs of Justin's eyes. In that moment, Justin knew he'd never love anyone else. This man was the one for him.

§♠

VON WASTED no time carrying Justin to bed. Now he couldn't stop toying with the man's fingers. Even with millions on the table, Von hadn't been sure he had enough to offer Justin to convince the man to leave everything for him.

"How long until you have to be in Phoenix?"

Von winced. "Two weeks."

"Two... Are you kidding me? I can't be ready to move in two weeks. My house, job, all those things need to be taken care of. I have to sell the house and I'm under contract at work."

Von could hear Justin's breaths coming faster with each word. "Take a breath, baby. It'll be okay. Phoenix isn't going anywhere. You take care of what you need to here, and I'll get us set up there. See? We're a team already."

A happy-sounding hum came from the back of Justin's

throat, letting Von know he liked hearing that. "It could take months for me to get everything tied up."

Von released a dramatic sigh. "I suppose you're worth the wait."

"Ugh," Justin groaned while trying to pinch him. "You suppose?"

A low chuckle escaped Von as he easily held Justin's wrists locked together, saving his hide from any pinching damage. "Stop. You know I'm completely in love with you. I'll be busy, trying to find my place with a new team. As much as I'll miss you, it might be best if you're a little behind me. I'd hate for you to get bored in a new town."

Justin's spine bowed as he fought against Von's hold. "You'd rather I be bored without you in a familiar town?"

Shifting positions, Von released Justin's hands as he covered the man's body with his own. He held Justin's gaze. "Tell me you love me."

"I love you," Justin said without hesitation.

"Trust me, okay? I'll take care of you. If you get bored, meet me on FaceTime and I'll get you off."

Justin's legs brushed Von's. He writhed beneath Von, making Von's dick stir. "What about now? How do you intend to keep me entertained?"

"How about a story?"

"Mmm," Justin hummed, obviously believing this story would be sexual.

Von settled in, bracing his weight so he wouldn't squash Justin but could continue holding him. "Once upon a time."

"Oooh, I love that. Very original."

Von winked. "Actually, it was almost a year ago, but that doesn't have the same ring to it." Von sucked in a deep breath when Justin laughed. The sound vibrated against his skin, making Von's body sing. He cleared his throat. "Anyhow, a year ago, I got hit in the back of the thigh with a stick during a game. He hit me full speed too, so no amount of padding could spare me from the blow. It left one hell of a bruise. After the game, I hobbled back to my room. All my teammates were off nursing their pride from our loss. All I wanted was to be with you."

"Awww."

A smile tugged at Von's lips, but he didn't stop. "I fell facedown across the bed, trying to ignore the pain in my thigh. It had been a month since the last time I saw you. As usual, you stopped texting me the moment the season started, and I was traveling all the time."

"I'm sorry."

Von shook his head at Justin's apology. "That's not the point of this story. I caved and called you because I couldn't stand another second of not hearing your voice. You answered, but you couldn't play because you were working late."

"I remember that night," Justin said, interrupting him. "I expected you to be disappointed I couldn't meet you on FaceTime. Instead, you asked me to read the notes I had to finish aloud."

"You read to me until I fell asleep," Von finished for him. "That's the night I realized I was in love with you."

Justin's expression transformed, sobering. His gaze moved over Von's face, as if searching for the truth. "Then why the thing with Luka?"

He could tell it bothered Justin to ask, but Von was relieved he had. His few dates with Luka still stood between them, even if Justin never brought up the incident. Von hadn't given Justin much time to think tonight, but eventually, he would. When he did, he'd realize Von would be working for Luka soon, and the shit would hit the fan if they didn't talk about everything now.

"Whether Luka ever admits it or not, he was using me to deal with losing the man he loved. I was pissed off because you acted like it didn't matter if I was in your life. Luka was safe because I knew it was only a matter of time before his man snapped over Luka being seen with me. I was right. They're now happily married and I'm where I'm supposed to be. You were right to be angry with me over those dates, but I've never been good with handling my emotions. The way I feel about you isn't immune to my ineptitude." Von pushed Justin's hair out of his face and forced the man to hold his stare. "I'll fail you again. It's bound to happen, but I can promise you it won't be in the form of cheating. Not only do I not have time for anyone else, there's no one else like you, and you're the only one for me."

"Will you make love to me now?" Justin whispered, melting Von's heart. "I don't want this moment to end."

Von slid his hand up Justin's thigh, before lifting the man's leg higher and probing Justin's ass with his cock. "This will never end," Von said, making Justin a vow. They were too perfect for one another. Nothing could ever come between them.

6

Two months later...

*J*ustin: How was your day?

    Justin: I'm guessing it was busy since you're not answering.

Justin: Guess I'll go to bed.

ॐ

VON: Shit. I'm sorry. My phone was in my locker. You're probably in bed by now.

ॐ

JUSTIN: It's okay. I'm sure there'll be days we'll miss each other.

    Justin: Seems today is another of those days.

ॐ

VON: Goddamn it. I turned my phone off for a team meeting and forgot to turn it back on.

❧

JUSTIN: It's no problem.

❧

VON: You only have a few more weeks until the move. I cannot wait. All this not getting to see you fucking sucks.

Von: Damn. I just noticed the time. Guess I missed you again.

❧

VON: Maybe don't watch the news today.

Justin: Why?

Von: Hey, I actually caught you. I miss you.

Justin: I miss you too.

Von: I love you.

It couldn't have been more obvious that Von was avoiding telling him why he shouldn't watch the news. Justin dialed his number, refusing to let the man wiggle out of telling him. It rang once before Von's sexy accent filled the line.

"Hey."

"Hey, yourself," Justin said, hearing the breathless note to his voice. "I love you too. Why am I not supposed to watch the news?"

Silence met Justin's question. Justin's stomach muscles twisted. A horrible feeling overcame him. When Von finally responded, his reluctant tone didn't make Justin feel any better. "Years ago, I dated this ref. It didn't last long and nothing came of it, obviously. Now, it seems someone—angry over me changing teams—leaked a photo of us together. Since it's me, I can glance at the photo and tell it's old, but this guy is trying to claim I'm still seeing the official, which would break a ton of rules. It's bullshit and won't amount to anything, but I don't want it hurting us, you know?"

A wave of relief washed over Justin. "Oh, is that all? That's no big deal. I would've known that wasn't true without you telling me." Justin massaged his forehead as he made the claim.

"Are you sure? You don't sound sure."

A chuckle escaped Justin. "I'm positive."

"You're not upset?"

"Nope," Justin said as he shifted positions and stretched out on the couch. His body felt heavy—like an invisible weight pressed down on him. He'd tell Von tomorrow about his house selling. Von had too much on his plate right now. Maybe he'd surprise Von by showing up in Phoenix early.

"I fucking love you."

Another laugh slipped from Justin. "I fucking love you too. I'm not feeling great today," Justin confessed.

"You sound tired. Maybe you should go to bed early? You've been working too hard, trying to get all the loose ends tied up for the move. Now that you've finally worked your last day, it's all catching up with you."

"Probably."

"You feel so far away."

Justin's chest tightened. "Give it a few weeks and you'll be tired of having me under your feet."

"Never." The conviction in Von's tone had a smile

tugging at the corners of his mouth. "I'm sorry, baby, but I have to head out if I want to make it to the arena on time."

"Okay. I'll be watching to see you win."

"Go to bed," Von ordered. "No one will judge you."

"If you say so."

"I say so," Von said, his voice turning sultry. "I love you, baby. I'll be thinking about you."

"Think about winning," Justin argued. "And I love you too. Bye, sweetie."

"Bye, babe."

For a full ten minutes, Justin considered moving to the bed. His body wouldn't cooperate. Instead, he stared at the ceiling and tried catching his breath. Damn, he couldn't remember the last time he was this exhausted. He should be elated. Today had been his last day on the job. Tomorrow, he'd start the process of moving to Phoenix. Justin was only days away from the rest of his life. Maybe Von was right. He'd taken on too much alone. Once he settled in to his new life, he'd have all the time in the world to relax. His phone rang again. He glanced at it. He couldn't avoid his mom's call. She'd worry.

"Hello?"

"What's this about Von dating someone else?"

Justin massaged the spot in his chest where a new ache bloomed. "Von isn't dating anyone else."

"Your father says there's a picture of him on that sports app thing he uses of Von with another man."

"Look at the picture. It's old."

"Let me see that photo," Kate ordered. Her voice sounded distant as if she held the phone away. Justin breathed through his nose while he waited. Jesus. He really didn't feel right. "Oh, yeah, I see what you're saying. That's a super-old picture of Von. No one will fall for that."

Justin sat up, prepared to remind his mom she'd called because she'd fallen for it. His head spun. The pain in his chest increased. A sharp pain began in his jaw and crawled its way down his arm. "Mom, I think I need to go to the hospital. Something isn't right."

"Oh my god. What's wrong? Never mind. Hang up and call 911. I'll try to find a way to get there."

"You stay there. You can't afford a trip right now with Dad being on dialysis. I'll let you know what I find out."

"Stop arguing with me and call an ambulance. I love you."

"Love you too," Justin slurred, hoping he could hold out for help.

⁂

THE ICE under Von's skates seemed smoother tonight. It was like he couldn't fail. Every move he made—golden. It was a high-scoring game as far as hockey went. If he wasn't having the best game of his life, it might've been boring, considering they were blowing out the competition.

He'd expected tonight would be a nightmare. Between the massive contract he'd been awarded and the new scandal attached to his name, he'd gotten the side eye from more than one player before hitting the ice. Now Von would solidify his spot—prove he was worth every dime. Von hadn't gotten here by accident. He'd worked his ass off for years, taking part in grueling training sessions since he was five years old. Von would be damned if he let a nasty rumor make his sacrifices or talent seem less. He'd earned this spot.

They easily won six to one. Von's muscles burned from the effort. His chest heaved as he fought to catch his breath.

He strained to give the reporter a play-by-play as he gasped for air between each word, but he'd won star player for the game. Von couldn't and wouldn't back down from the honor.

He lost count of how many people slapped him across the back before he made it back to his locker. His first thought was to call Justin and share his excitement. Luka appeared over his shoulder before Von could turn his phone on.

"Great game."

Von smiled as he met Luka's green gaze. "Thanks. Everything fell into place."

Luka wasn't smiling. That detail struck Von as odd. They'd won. Von had proven Luka hadn't made a mistake by offering for him. The man's team was off to a great start. That meant lots of money for Luka.

"I don't want to ruin your celebration. Go out, enjoy your victory. Then I need you in my office by eight a.m. tomorrow."

Luka's tone chilled Von's blood. "Okay. Is everything all right?"

"I hope it will be," Luka said, doing nothing to calm the terror rising in Von's chest. "Enjoy your night. See me in the morning," Luka ordered before walking away. Von fought the urge to call the man back and beg him to tell him everything now. He had no intention of celebrating. Von would much rather Luka put him out of his misery.

Von rushed through his shower. He turned down several offers to hit the town before he made it to his car. Once there, Von closed himself inside the silent vehicle, letting the quiet and darkness engulf him. Justin hadn't been feeling well. That wasn't the only thing stopping Von from calling him. This was one thing too much to Von's mind. One scandal too many.

First, he'd spent two years expecting Justin to wait around—be available when he sailed back in to town. Then, he'd flaunted another man in his face by going on those dates with Luka. He'd asked the man to give up everything and move to the opposite side of the country. Hell, Von wasn't sure he'd once stopped to truly consider Justin's feelings about any of it. On paper, Von was a genius, but he never thought outside his bubble. He'd seen the opportunity of a lifetime, playing for Phoenix, and he'd taken it. He'd assumed Justin would be thrilled to quit working at a job in a town he'd strove for his entire life. In truth, Von was an ass.

Not once had he asked what Justin wanted out of life. Von was damn certain it wasn't Justin's dream to be stuck with some guy whose face always ended up on the news in photos with someone else. When would he stop humiliating Justin at every turn? It was like he couldn't get enough of grinding Justin under his heel.

By the time Von fired his truck to life, he'd discovered a whole new level of self-hatred. With every new dark thought, Von's black mood deepened until there was no reasoning with himself. Everything he touched always turned to shit. No one should be saddled with him, especially someone as sweet and as amazing Justin. Von was a walking, selfish disaster. How could he embarrass Justin like this? Fuck. Hadn't Justin made it clear how he'd felt when pictures of Von with Luka had surfaced? Now here he was again. Goddamn it. Someone should save Justin from him before it was too late.

THE EGGSHELL-COLORED WALLS of the hospital room he'd been assigned only had one bright spot. Justin stared at it. There was a picture of flowers that were an odd shade of pink staring back at Justin. His gaze had fixed upon the picture the moment his mom had gone into full-on panic mode. That was where he'd zoned out. This was a familiar conversation. She wanted to be here with Justin, but she needed to be there in Tennessee with Justin's dad. Not to mention, she couldn't afford the trip. In her aggravation, she'd resorted to her usual rant about Justin moving so far away.

"Mom, you don't have to come here," Justin argued for the hundredth time. "They put in a Vena Cava filter. It'll catch any more blood clots that form. This shouldn't happen again."

Kate sighed, sounding defeated. "You just feel so far away. I never thought, when you moved away, we'd run into this problem one day. It used to cost nothing to catch a quick flight. Now you can't go anywhere without it costing an arm and a leg. I fucking hate this."

"I know, Mom, but I'm okay. This will pass, and I'll come see you as soon as I can."

"Is Von there yet?"

Justin swallowed past the lump forming in his throat. Jesus, he wished Von was there. "I tried calling earlier, but there was no answer. It's hockey season, you know? There's no more sense in him coming than you. He has a schedule to keep to right now."

"I know, but I just wish someone was there with you. No one should have to be alone in the hospital."

"It's okay," Justin said, hoping to reassure her. "I have a friend coming."

"Do you? Or are you just saying that so I'll quit fussing over you?"

Justin smiled. His mom knew him well, but in this case, he wasn't only trying to appease her. Hawke had called, wanting to do lunch while he was passing through. Once he'd learned Justin was in the hospital, there was nothing Justin could say to convince the man not to come. "I'm being one hundred percent honest. I won't be alone."

Kate blew out a sigh. "All right. As long as you're not alone, I guess I can survive not being there this one time."

Justin's shoulders fell. Relief coursed through him. "Thank you. I'll keep you posted."

"Okay. I love you, baby."

"I love you too," Justin said before disconnecting the call.

The moment Justin set his phone aside, the door burst open and twenty balloons shoved their way inside. Only around half of them said "Get Well." The other half were birthday balloons. After much fighting to get them all shoved through the doorway, Jamie's smiling face appeared from behind the explosion of color.

"I brought happiness," Jamie announced. Hawke stepped inside behind him. Jamie nodded the man's way. "Not him. I meant the balloons. Hawke is my happiness. Most of these are birthday balloons because the store I sent my bodyguard into didn't have much else. I figured, what the hell, you had to have had a birthday at some point that I missed. So get well and happy belated and or early birthday." A laugh snuck out. Justin immediately regretted it. Who knew having a catheter shoved up the vein in your leg could be so painful. "Oh," Jamie said, opening the door again. "I forgot the doc was on our heels. Guess I shut the door in his face. Oops."

Dr. Meyers stepped inside the room, looking more than

a little baffled by the mess that was Jamie. The man had most likely been standing in the hall, afraid to come in until after Jamie left.

"Hiya, doc," Jamie said, closing the door behind Dr. Meyers before offering the closest chair to Hawke and going in search of his own.

"Hello," Dr. Meyers said, dragging out the word before focusing on Justin. "Why are there security guards posted outside your door? For a minute there, I wasn't sure I should come in."

Jamie wiggled his fingers. "Those are mine."

Justin bit his lip to keep from laughing.

Dr. Meyers focused on him once more. "How are you feeling?"

"Like I got hit by a fast-moving truck," Justin said, answering honestly.

The doctor felt Justin's abdomen and listened to his heart before responding. "I'm not surprised. Are you having any pain?"

"Not really. I'm just sore. More than anything, I'm curious. How did this happen? It's been months since my surgery. Why did I have another clot?"

The doctor draped his stethoscope around his neck. "We're still running tests."

But he had an idea. Justin could see it in the man's eyes. He could tell by the way the man carefully avoided making eye contact. "I would prefer if you'd be honest with me. Most people might need you to feed them bullshit, but I'm an information is power kind of guy. If you think you're about to tell me something bad, let me be prepared to hear it."

Dr. Meyers blew out a sigh, and Justin knew. It was bad. "After your last clot, we didn't do a lot of testing, because clots after surgery are common. At your follow-up visit, we did run a couple of tests to ensure you weren't suffering from some form of genetic or acquired hypercoagulation. So we've already ruled that out. This time, the clot was random and your white blood cell count is extremely high."

"Which means?"

Dr. Meyers held his gaze. "Most likely? Cancer."

The air left Justin's lungs. He clenched his hands to keep from showing his feelings. Cancer. Fuck. Justin cleared his throat. "What kind of cancer?"

The doctor shook his head. "There are several types of cancer that cause your blood to clot. Really, just about any cancer can cause your blood to react in such a way. We won't know until we go looking."

Justin nodded, trying his ass off to hang on to his shit. "Okay. If it's there, let's find it."

Dr. Meyers patted Justin's knee. "Chances are good, considering your lack of any other symptoms, we've caught whatever this is in its earliest stages. We'll figure it out."

"All right." Justin's voice sounded every bit as numb as he felt.

"I'll check in on you later."

Justin nodded. He waited until the man was gone before glancing Hawke and Jamie's way. They both appeared every bit as stunned as Justin imagined he did. "Thank you for the balloons."

"Where's Von?" Jamie asked, ignoring Justin's thanks.

"He's—" Justin's cell phone rang, cutting him off. He glanced down. It was Von. "There he is now."

Jamie stood. "We'll leave you alone while you answer that. Would you like something from the cafeteria?"

Justin shook his head and answered the phone. He hadn't realized until he was moments away from hearing

Von's voice, how much he needed Von. His arms felt heavy and empty. There was a weight sitting on his chest, suffocating him. Justin wished Von could hold him and tell him everything would be all right. He needed Von to make this better. "Hey."

"Have you seen the news yet?"

Von's question caught him off guard. "No. I told you yesterday I wasn't worried about all that. Listen, I—"

"They've suspended me, pending a full investigation," Von said, cutting him off. "It seems dating a league official is a serious no-no, no matter how long ago it was."

He'd never heard Von sound so dead. "What?"

"Yep. I've already hired a lawyer. That's why I'm so late calling you back. They suspended me this morning, and I went straight to my lawyer's office. You called a few times. Is everything okay?"

"Um." Justin didn't know what to say. He didn't want to add to Von's burden, but damn, Justin had never felt more alone and adrift. He opened his mouth, searching for something that would bring Von to his side while not making the man's life harder.

Von cut him off. "I've been thinking." Justin snapped his teeth together and held his breath. There was something in Von's tone. "In the past two years, I've put you through a lot."

"It was nothing I couldn't handle." Justin wondered why he sounded so calm. His doctor had definitely said cancer. Von had been suspended. Now, there was something wrong with Von's voice. It sounded hard—like he'd closed himself off from Justin.

"You shouldn't have to handle it," Von snapped before blowing out a breath, as if he fought to keep his temper under control. "Look, I don't think you should move here after all." Everything inside Justin's brain came to a screeching halt. All he could do was listen as Von destroyed him. "They could have this mess cleared up by tomorrow, but I doubt it, and I don't want your name dragged through the mud alongside mine. I can't focus on this and you."

"Okay." Even Justin didn't understand why his brain sifted through all the possible reactions and spit that one word out.

"We're not over for good. I swear it."

Yeah, they were. Justin just didn't have the energy to argue. "All right."

"I promise I will make everything better later. Right now, I just can't."

"I understand." Really, he did. Maybe Von loved Justin, but he didn't love Justin as much as he loved himself. He couldn't breathe. There wasn't enough oxygen in the room. Yesterday morning, Justin had woken to a bright future. He'd been moving to Phoenix and spending the rest of his life with Von. Now, he had nothing left and might not live long enough for it to matter. Maybe Von was right? Maybe it was all for the best?

"If you don't want to wait for me while I get this sorted, I'll understand." Von kept saying words, and Justin wanted it to stop. Why was he prolonging this?

"Hopefully, everything will work out for you. You deserve all the best things in life." Justin wasn't sure if he meant it. He just wanted the call to end.

"Will you be okay?"

Fuck. Justin didn't know how much more he could stand. "Sure. Jamie and Hawke are here. I have to go." Without waiting for a response, Justin disconnected the call. He stared at the face of his phone and tried hard not to think. He clicked on Von's name and blocked him. They were over. Time no longer held meaning. That was Justin's only excuse for having no clue how much time passed before Jamie and Hawke reappeared.

Despite having told them he didn't want anything, Hawke handed him a sandwich and a bag of chips. "I know you said you didn't want anything, and this probably isn't great, but it's bound to be better than whatever they've been giving you."

Justin set the food aside without meeting anyone's gaze. He was afraid if anyone looked at him too closely, he'd fall apart. "Thank you."

"When will Von be here?"

Justin kept his gaze locked on the opposite wall as he answered Jamie's question. "Never."

"What?" Jamie sounded every bit as incredulous as a friend should. Justin couldn't feel anything past the pain. His eyes stung and his chest hurt. He'd never felt emptier in his life. "You're in the hospital and you need him right now. Is there not a protocol in place for players who have family emergencies?"

"It doesn't matter." Justin clutched the sheets and prayed he wouldn't cry. If he'd ever felt lower, he couldn't remember it. "I'm not family. Plus..." He swallowed. The words were on his tongue and once they fell, they'd be out there—in the universe and killing him. Justin took a breath. There was no avoiding it. "He dumped me."

Jamie sucked in an audible breath. "What. The. Actual. Fuck?"

Justin still couldn't look at anyone. "I think I'd kind of like to go to sleep now."

Hawke moved his chair closer to the bed. "You do that," he said, rubbing Justin's arm and almost tearing apart the last seam holding Justin together. "We'll be here when you wake up."

Justin closed his eyes and prayed he wouldn't wake at all. "Thanks. I'm sorry I'm not better company."

"Fuck that," Jamie muttered. "Just go to sleep."

THE INSTANT JUSTIN'S eyes opened, reality slammed into his chest. There was no slow build-up—a moment of peace before he remembered. Everything he'd lost and stood to lose waited to overtake him at the first second of leaving his dreams. It had been that way every time he'd opened his eyes in the last week since Von destroyed him. Justin's gaze landed on Jamie and Hawke. They hadn't left him since he'd gotten the news. The only time either man stepped from the room was to go in hunt of food or some other necessity. Even then, only one would leave—like they were scared for Justin to be alone. They may've had a point. Justin was a bit scared of himself too. No one could contain this much rage and live to tell about it.

At some point during the day, Jamie must have pulled the chair out into a cot, giving Hawke a place to sleep with his head resting in Jamie's lap. They were such a beautiful couple. The sight of Jamie brushing his fingers through a sleeping Hawke's hair had even Justin's dead heart smiling. Since Jamie had been hanging around Justin's hospital room, he couldn't remember a single moment when the man behaved in the same outrageous way as he had the first night they'd met.

"You've been very subdued," Justin said, bringing Jamie's head up. He didn't seem surprised to see Justin awake or ashamed over getting caught caressing his husband.

Jamie flashed him a sweet smile. "Believe it or not, this is the real me. Being obnoxious is a nervous tic for me. I calm down once I get to know people."

"That's an odd nervous tic." Justin was simply making conversation—filling the deadness in his heart with empty talk.

Jamie shrugged and went back to watching his fingers slip through Hawke's hair. "I'm an orphan. Growing up, I bounced from foster home to foster home. No one wanted me for long. I learned how to read people's needs. Sometimes, if I could make people laugh, they'd keep me a little longer. Other times, I had to bleed into the background, so I wouldn't get separated from my twin. Still, no one wanted me forever. Some things you don't grow out of, I guess." He traced Hawke's jawline. "He's the only person who's ever kept me and wanted me for who I am."

Justin's chest hurt from watching them, but he couldn't look away. "Tell me more. I want to hear the story." They made an ugly world seem a little less hopeless.

Jamie didn't look up. "When I fell in love with Hawke, he was dating a friend of mine. It might sound crazy, but I was cool with it, because he was happy. Still, I swore if he ever gave me hope, I'd dog his heels to the end of time."

"What happened?" Justin didn't know why he whispered the question. Their love weaved a spell he didn't want to break.

Jamie met his gaze. "He gave me hope." Hawke snagged Jamie's hand and kissed it before holding it to his chest like a security blanket. Jamie smiled. The sight made Justin's eyes sting. "He's still asleep," Jamie said, as if assuring Justin their chat wasn't disturbing his husband. "He kisses me in his sleep all the time."

A lump rose in Justin's throat. "You're both very lucky."

"Just me, actually," Jamie said, sounding as if he truly

believed that. "Hawke's getting the life he deserves because I won't let it be any other way for him. If he told me tomorrow that my career made him unhappy, then tomorrow would be the day I never sang another note."

"He'd never say that. When he talks about you, I can hear the pride in his voice. It would kill him if you gave up music."

For a full minute, Jamie stared at him expressionless.

Justin couldn't take the way the man's knowing gaze moved over his face. He nodded toward Hawke. "Being here is wearing him out. I'll understand if you'd like to get out of here. Promise. I'm used to being alone."

Jamie shook his head. "It's the tour that's wearing him out. Not you. This is the biggest one I've ever done, but it'll probably be my last for a long while. I don't want to leave Hawke alone with a new baby and we sure as shit aren't taking a baby on the road."

A genuine smile pulled at the corners of Justin's mouth. "You're having a baby?"

Jamie nodded. "All the papers are in order. We're just waiting for our daughter to finish cooking. She'll be in here in about four months."

"Wow. How nervous are you?" Justin had no idea where the question came from. He only knew—if he was in Jamie's position—he'd be biting his nails and losing his hair.

"I'm fucking terrified," Jamie said, taking him by surprise. "Mostly that something will go wrong or fall through at the last minute and rip Hawke's heart out." Jamie smiled. "But also, there's guys like me out there and I might have to kill some fuckboi one of these days."

Justin snorted. He did not envy Jamie's position.

Jamie's smile fell. "What about you? Are you scared?"

Since Jamie had been real with him, Justin knew he

deserved the same. He thought it over before responding. "I'm angry. Seriously. I'm more pissed off than I've been in my whole life." Once the truth gate opened, Justin couldn't stop. "I quit my job and sold my house. Now I have to start my life over, except now I don't know how long that life will be. Fuck. I'm just mad."

Jamie nodded as if he understood, and Justin got the feeling Jamie truly did get it. "You deserve better than you got from Von."

Justin tried working up a smile. He failed. "It's not like I can compete with a dream career and a forty-two-million-dollar contract. Not that I would've asked him to choose me. No way could I live with knowing anyone sacrificed that much for me. I can't say it wouldn't have been nice if he'd dumped me before I gave up everything for him. It definitely would've been awesome if he hadn't kicked me while I was down." A bitter smile tugged at Justin's lips. "I think this was it for me, though. This is the broken heart that won't heal."

"They say time heals all wounds."

"They say a lot of shit that isn't true," Justin shot back. "Do you think you'd survive Hawke leaving?"

Jamie didn't answer. He didn't have to. Justin knew the answer by simply seeing them together. Neither Jamie nor Hawke would survive without the other.

Justin forced a fake smile. "Anyhow, I don't intend to curl into a ball and die. I'm just done with caring about people. People are a huge disappointment." Life was every man for himself, only to be shared when it was convenient to do so. Von had taught him that. It was a hard-learned lesson, but Von had finally driven the point home.

7

*T*here was a bite to the winter air. Von imagined the nights were probably downright cold here already. Back in Phoenix, Von probably would've had to wait until February for the weather to cool down. Here, it felt great in the daytime. Von wondered if the weather was a sign he was making the right decision. As if the universe heard him and decided to hand him another clue he was on the right track, he spotted the grocery store where he'd first met Justin.

Von changed lanes. They sold flowers there. Surely flowers would help his case when he fell on his knees and begged Justin to forgive him... again. It seemed eleven a.m. was the time to shop for groceries. There was no more than a handful of cars parked in the lot. He parked in the second space directly in front of the entrance. As he climbed from his truck, he eyed the Lotus parked next to him. It was sweet. Its body was the orange and black combo he'd thought about buying for himself. He almost got away with eye fucking a stranger's vehicle. Before he could move away, he found his path blocked by Jamie. Von was hard pressed to decide which of them was more surprised to see the other.

"What are you doing here?"

The hostility in Jamie's question caught Von off guard. He glanced around, seeking any clue to Jamie's anger. His gaze landed on Hawke. Damn, the man's green eyes were even more beautiful in the sunlight, but they too held a hint of hatred Von never expected. A large chocolate-skinned male who matched Von in size stood at Hawke's back. Von dismissed him as part of Jamie's security team. He focused on Jamie once more. "I dropped by to grab Justin some flowers. Is there some reason I shouldn't shop here? Wait. Are they selling used bath water and calling it spring water?" Von asked, hoping to tease the fury from Jamie's expression. Normally, jokes always won over Jamie.

Jamie's brow furrowed. "I don't mean here, here," Jamie said, motioning toward the store. "I mean here, here," he said, pointing at the ground. "Like here in South Carolina."

Von felt his face screw up in his confusion. "This is where Justin lives. Where else would I be?"

To Von's surprise, Jamie's temper snapped. "You'd be in hell if there was any justice in the world."

Von blinked at the sudden rage flying his way "Whoa."

"Jamie," Hawke said, obviously hoping to call his husband under control.

Von kept his gaze locked on Jamie. "Did I miss something?"

Jamie shook his head as if he couldn't believe Von's gall. "You're the dumbest genius I've ever met." Jamie seemed to think it over, before adding, "Not that I've met many geniuses."

"Wow. Don't hold back." Even Von heard the sarcasm in

his tone, but either Jamie chose to ignore it or Von's words suited his purposes because he kept talking.

"Okay, then. You're also the biggest jackass I've ever met, and that's really saying something. Do you have any idea how many people I meet in a day?"

Von felt his face screw up in confusion. He shook his head. "Did I do something to you?"

Jamie scratched his chin, being as obnoxious as possible. "Let me think. Hmmm. Do I feel your actions directly affected me?" He straightened and threw off all appearances of joking. "Yeah, I guess in a way, I do. I don't like it when people give me the feels. Nobody gives me the fucking feels but my husband. But damn, man, it was hard as hell to hold my shit together, sitting there with Justin while the doctor told him he had cancer. Then, this is the best part of the story, five minutes later, you call and dump him." Von couldn't fucking breathe. He thought he might be having a heart attack, but Jamie was nowhere near finished. "Oh, and let's not forget—"

"Jamie, maybe we should stay out of it," Hawke said, cutting him off.

Jamie went back to pretending to think it over. "Nah. I think staying silent at the hospital was the extent of my business-minding abilities. Dude, he gave up his job. Sold his house. What the fuck did you think—"

"He sold his house?"

Jamie rolled his eyes. "Do you know any fucking thing about Justin or is everything always about you? Wait," Jamie said, holding up his hand. "Don't bother answering that. I already know."

Von ignored Jamie's open hatred. Nothing mattered as much as finding Justin. "If he sold his house, where's he staying?"

"Like I would tell you," Jamie shot back.

In spite of Jamie's anger, Von didn't stop pushing. "Please? I'm here because I want to fall on my knees and beg. I didn't know about the..." Von swallowed, because it hurt. "I didn't know about the cancer or the house. I knew he'd quit his job, but I'd planned to send him the money to cover everything." He stopped, recognizing he wasn't getting through to Jamie. "He's been ignoring my calls. I need to find him."

A muscle in Jamie's jaw ticked. He stared Von down, obviously intent on holding his ground.

"He's at Geeks Unlimited," Hawke said behind Jamie.

Von's chin shot up, meeting Hawke's gaze. "What?"

Hawke motioned toward a strip mall next to the store where they stood. "Geeks Unlimited. It's a computer repair shop slash electronics store. That's where Justin is right now."

Hope lit in Von's chest. Jamie still stared at him with hatred in his eyes and Hawke didn't look any happier about handing over the information, but Von didn't care. He had what he needed. "Thanks for being here for him," Von said, hoping to extend the first olive branch, but he couldn't stop from adding, "I still wish you would've called me and let me know what was happening."

Jamie's gaze slid his way. "Would it have made a difference? You made your choice, and it wasn't Justin."

Jamie opened the passenger side door of the ultra-expensive car and motioned Hawke inside. Hawke moved to slide inside. With one foot inside the car, Hawke met his gaze. "For the record, I didn't tell you where Justin is so you can make things right. Personally, I don't think you deserve him. But Justin deserves closure, and the chance to spit in your face," Hawke added before turning his back on Von and sliding inside the car.

Von never considered arguing his case. All he wanted was to get to Justin before the man disappeared. Justin was a get in and get what he needed and get out type of guy when it came to shopping. If he was at an electronics store, he might not be there much longer. He could've walked, but he didn't have time. Instead, he fired his truck to life and cut through the parking lot before snagging the closest space. He searched the lot for Justin's car but didn't see it. Von's heart rate kicked up. What if he was already gone? He didn't know where the man lived any longer. Von doubted he'd get any further answers from Jamie or Hawke. Maybe they'd dropped Justin off, and that was how they knew where he was?

With his panic rising by the moment, Von rushed inside. Thankfully, it wasn't a huge place. He spotted Justin right away. Even with Justin's head covered by a stocking cap, Von knew it was him. It was as if his body was attuned to Justin. He could find the man in any crowd. Von's panic disappeared, replaced with confusion. Justin wore a royal blue polo with the store's logo on the sleeve—like every other employee inside the store. His feet moved in Justin's direction. He didn't stop until no more than two feet separated them. His hands itched to touch the man he'd missed with everything he possessed. It felt like forever since the last time he saw him.

Von thought of all the many things he needed to say. He opened his mouth, intent on pleading for Justin to forgive him—to love him again. "What are you doing working in an electronics store?"

Justin went still. He didn't turn right away. When he did, his face was clear of all surprise or emotion of any kind. For all the pep talks Von gave himself, there was no way he could've prepared himself for seeing Justin again. The dark circles under the man's eyes were new. He'd also lost weight he couldn't spare. There was a hard edge to his eyes that hadn't been there before. All those things were Von's fault. There wasn't enough penance in the world.

Rather than telling Von to fuck off, as Von expected, Justin surprised him by answering. "Well, since I'd quit my job to move to Phoenix, and no longer had health insurance when I found out—" Justin paused, as if stopping himself before he told too much. He started again. "When I had a medical emergency, here I am. I'm now working two jobs, hoping not to completely wreck my credit while I try to fight my way out from underneath a couple of hundred thousand dollars' worth of medical debt that's all soon to be headed for collection. Thanks for asking. Unless you're here to get your computer fixed, I need to get back to work."

It was the same as getting kicked in the throat. Von had no excuse for a lot of things, but the medical bills hadn't even occurred to him. "I'll take care of your bills tomorrow."

Justin laughed. There wasn't an ounce of humor in the gesture. In fact, Von had never heard an uglier sound. "It must be so nice to be you. All guilt removed with the swipe of a debit card." He motioned as if swiping a card. "Cha-ching. Every sin wiped clean. Go fuck yourself, Von. I don't want your money." As if lending truth to his words, Justin walked away.

Von wasn't having it. He stayed on Justin's heels. "Where's your car? I didn't see it outside."

While keeping his eyes locked on the clipboard in his hand, Justin made notes as he answered. "Jamie dropped me off today. I had a doctor's appointment and I always feel bad after..." Justin snapped his teeth together as if loath to say more.

"That was nice of Jamie," Von said for lack of anything more. This was bad. He didn't know how to fix this. His eyes burned. He wanted to hold Justin—tell him everything would be all right, but Justin wouldn't even look at him.

"It was nice. The man has this huge tour happening right now, and a hundred other things going on his life, yet he's able to deal with me and all of that." Justin met Von's gaze. "Imagine that," he said, looking away again.

He deserved that dig, but it didn't mean Von would go away. "I'm here now. He can get back to his tour."

"There's no socializing on the clock," a guy who looked to be sixteen said, interrupting them.

Von glanced over, more than ready to get Justin fired if it meant he could have his say. "Look, dude—"

"Oh, wow. You're Von Wolf. Could I get your autograph?" the dude asked.

Even though Von could feel Justin's glare biting into his skin, he didn't glance Justin's way as he used the situation to his advantage. Von pasted on his most winning smile. "I'd be more than happy to sign whatever you'd like..."

"Charlie," the man supplied.

Von nodded. "I'd be happy to sign whatever you like, Charlie if I can steal Justin away for the day. See, I'm having an issue with my home entertainment system, and he's the only person I trust in my house."

Charlie nodded. "Of course. Someone like you wouldn't want strangers invading your home. I'm cool with you stealing Justin for the day, but I'll still have to charge you for his time."

Von nodded. "I wouldn't expect anything less."

Justin was seething. Von could feel the hatred rolling off

the man in waves, but he didn't argue. What could he say? Von had backed him in a corner. If Justin needed his job as much as he claimed, he wouldn't do anything to damage it. However, Von would make damn sure his man didn't have to ever come back to this place again.

☙

JUSTIN WAS TORN between feeling resigned and ready to cry. He was so tired—more exhausted than he'd ever been in his life. It seemed he should've been surprised to see Von there, but he wasn't. Everything sucked, so it only seemed fair Von should show up to kick Justin some more while he was down. He watched Von signing autographs. For a moment, he even considered making a run for it. He could call a cab. Most likely, if he texted Jamie or Hawke, the pair would come back for him. Instead, Justin stood there and waited.

Von had gotten bigger. Justin marveled over that fact. If he'd thought about it, Justin would've thought the man would've lost some muscle, considering he hadn't been playing these past few months. Justin had tried damn hard not to think about Von at all. Sometimes, when he was at his weakest, Justin's brain would dredge up a memory of Von— the way he smelled or the way it felt when Von would hold him. Justin always shut those thoughts down before they took hold and killed him. Before Von, Justin hadn't known it was possible to hate someone and love someone so much at the same time.

Von finished up and turned his sexy gaze Justin's way. Justin wanted to vomit. "You ready?"

"Do I have a choice?" Justin muttered under his breath as Von steered him toward the door.

"You always have a choice," Von said as he opened the

passenger side door for Justin. "But no matter what you do, I'll follow," Von promised as he closed the door, shutting Justin inside the truck.

Justin's traitorous gaze followed Von as he circled the front of the truck. He wanted to punch him in the balls for being so hot. If there was any justice in the world, Von would be as ugly on the outside as he was inside. If anyone knew how unfair life was, it was Justin. Von was only one of the many ways life had fucked Justin. He'd always believed by the time he made it to thirty, he would have all his shit together. Justin was thirty-two and further away from shit togetherness than he'd ever been in his life.

Von slid behind the wheel. For a moment, their gazes met. Justin narrowed his eyes before looking away. If he looked fucking childish, he couldn't be bothered to care. It was not like Von didn't know he shouldn't have come back here.

Justin stared out the window and tried to pretend he was somewhere else. Von wasn't there beside him. This wasn't happening to him. The truck crawled to a stop at a red light. He could see Von's reflection in the window. Each breath Justin took came harder than the last as he watched Von turn his head.

"I love you."

At Von's claim, Justin opened the door and got out. He couldn't fucking do this. They'd driven far enough away from his work that no one would know he hadn't gone with Von. The fucking bastard. He loved only himself. There was a bus stop down the road. Justin didn't know the schedule. He had no clue when the next bus ran or where it went, but any fucking thing was better than Von. He could hear Von cursing as he slammed the door. Justin didn't look back. He could call Jamie or Hawke. In fact, he could call a cab. There was no reason whatsoever for him to endure this.

Tires screeched behind him. Von took the corner fast before whipping into the pharmacy and parking. He was close enough Justin heard the man's door slam as he came after him. Justin picked up his pace. It didn't matter that he knew he was being ridiculous. Justin couldn't stop. He could hear Von's footsteps, proving how attuned he was to Von's every move. When the man's shadow almost overtook him, Justin spun, and lost it.

"I need you to go away from me," Justin said, hearing the desperation in his voice and unable to stop. "I know you don't care. You're so used to everyone giving you everything you want, but you have to hear me now. I need you to go away from me today."

Von put his hands out as if trying to placate Justin. "Let me take you home, and I promise to leave you alone for today." Justin wasn't stupid. He knew Von would keep to the exact letter of his word. He'd leave Justin alone for today, but tomorrow, he'd be back. "I get that you're sick—"

"How you do know that?" Justin snapped. "You shouldn't know that." Justin took a step toward Von as he yelled the words. He'd never wanted to physically fight someone as much as he did Von.

"My mistake," Von said, as if trying to calm a wild animal. Justin didn't doubt for a second he looked like one at the moment. "Blame me, okay? I ran into Jamie and Hawke at the store and they let it slip."

Justin wanted to stamp his feet and scream at the top of his lungs. He never wanted Von to know. "I guess I know why you're here now."

Von shook his head. "That's not true. I'd stopped at the store to buy you flowers and that's when I ran into them." He drew a cross on his chest. "Cross my heart, I was already on my way to see you. I'd already decided I couldn't live another day without you."

If Justin had been armed, Von would be dead already. He'd never been more enraged in his entire life. He didn't know a person could feel so much fury toward another person. Justin took another step toward Von. "How dare you say that to me? You don't deserve to get to say that to me."

"Justin, please get in the truck. If you don't want to talk, we won't, but let me get you home."

Without a word, Justin stomped his way back to the truck. He stood at the door and waited for Von to unlock the door. Instead of hitting the button on the key fob and letting Justin in, Von waited to hit the button until he could open the door for Justin. He scurried in, hoping Von wouldn't use this opportunity to touch him. Justin was scared what he might do if any part of Von came in contact with him.

Staying true to his word, Von didn't speak other than asking directions to Justin's house. As he gave them, Justin cursed himself as being ten shades of an idiot. Of course Von wanted to take him home, so he'd know where Justin lived now. He would've given the man the wrong address if it had occurred to him before he'd given Von the right one. The apartment he lived in now was a lot smaller than his house had been. Unfortunately, after using all the money he'd made selling his home on medical bills, he didn't have anything left but even more medical bills. Now, he was back to apartment living. It wasn't so bad. Only one of his neighbors had a dog that barked nonstop. The other made up for it by having screaming kids. He was also convinced the guy who lived above him had two wooden legs, causing him to stomp with every step he took, but otherwise, Justin got by.

Von pulled into the parking spot next to Justin's car and put the truck in park. "Justin, I—"

Justin leapt from the truck and slammed the door, cutting off whatever Von had been about to say. There was nothing Von could say to him that would change a damn thing. Von didn't pull away, even as Justin let himself in, but Justin didn't look back. If there was a god in heaven, Von would keep his word and leave Justin alone for at least a few hours. He wasn't equipped to deal with Von Wolf today. Justin needed time to think.

VON STARED at Justin's closed front door and tried not to think. This was so much worse than anything he'd imagined. Since Jamie had dropped the cancer bomb, Von had been going through the motions—concentrating on Justin. Now that he'd seen the hatred in Justin's exhausted gaze, Von was at a complete loss. Being an ass, he could fix by proving he'd never do it again. This... Von had nothing. The humane thing to do would be to fix all the monetary problems he'd created and get the hell out of Justin's life for good. Von couldn't do it. He'd already proven he was the worst sort of selfish bastard. Today was no different. He still loved Justin. Von couldn't stop.

He turned the keys in the ignition, shutting off the truck. There was no way he could leave. Justin wouldn't let him stay. The thing was—Von physically couldn't put the truck in reverse and drive away from Justin. His arms felt too heavy. He'd never been more heartsick in his life. No one would ever understand how badly he wished he'd been here. If anyone had given him a single clue, he didn't doubt for a second he would've been. The problem was—Justin would never believe any of that. So, Von would stay. Even if Justin wouldn't let him inside, Von would sit here until Justin let him make it right. All the calls he needed to make to pay off Justin's debt, Von could do right here from his cellphone. He had a car charger. No need to ever move again.

8

*A*fter the disastrous run in with Von, Justin had gone straight to bed, hoping a nap would clear his head. He hadn't slept at all. Instead, he'd stared at his bedroom ceiling and tortured himself. There wasn't a second of Von that Justin didn't remember. If he closed his eyes, he swore he could still feel Von's heat and smell the man's cologne. Each time he'd buried his nose against the crook of Von's neck still lived inside Justin's head. For the millionth time, Justin wished the love would die. His hatred was bigger now, but the love—goddamn that shit was still there, slowly killing him.

He checked his phone and noticed he'd missed a message from Jamie.

Jamie: *I went by your work and you were gone. Is everything okay?*

Fuck. He'd been so pissed off at Von, he'd forgotten to let Jamie know he didn't need to pick him up after work. Goddamn it. Hawke and Jamie had been so good to him. Justin growled. Von always made Justin lose his head. He shot a quick text off to Jamie.

Justin: *I'm SO sorry. Von showed up and gave me a ride home.*

Jamie: *Is everything okay? Do we need to help you hide the body? I can afford to get away with one murder.*

Justin smiled for the first time since seeing Von. Without Jamie and Hawke, Justin was scared to think what would've happened to him these past few months.

Justin: *No. I'm okay. That's a lie. I'm not okay, but I'll survive. I always do.*

Jamie: *We'll be around if you need us. I have a shovel and an alibi. I'm not afraid to use either.*

Justin: *Thank you. Love you guys.*

Jamie: *We love you too.*

They would be around for another two weeks and then the pair would have no choice but to head back across the pond. Jamie's tour was near its end and their baby would be arriving soon. They couldn't hold Justin's hand forever. In truth, he'd leaned on them for too long already. He was so weak. Sometimes, he sickened himself. Why couldn't he just deal with being alone? As if proving how weak he was, Justin scrolled through his contacts until he found Von's name. He unblocked him. The instant his finger hit the button, undoing three months of the wall he'd built, Justin hated himself for it. A sick pit of despair rose inside him.

The phone rang, pulling Justin from his misery. He checked the face of his cellphone. It was his mom. That gave Justin pause. Justin checked the time. His mom always called at the same time every day. Five hours had passed since Von had dropped him off. Justin blinked at the face of his phone. Had he really lain here, stewing for that long? Growling over his stupidity, Justin answered.

"Hello?"

"Hey, baby. How're you feeling today?"

Without thought, Justin drew a slow breath through his nose. He felt too many things to pick a single emotion. Instead, he lied. "I'm good. How are you?"

"Crazy busy, as always. Hey, sweetie, I need you to send me a list of who you owe and how much."

"Why?" Justin asked, taken aback by his mom's sudden interest.

"I want to help."

Justin sighed. "Mom, you're not in the position..." Suspicion sneaked in. "Wait. Did Von put you up to this?" The silence meeting Justin's question was all the answer he needed. "No. I don't want anything from Von."

"Baby, he's only trying to help, and he should. This is all his fault."

A snort escaped Justin. "Von is a piece of shit, but he didn't give me cancer."

"No," his mom agreed. "He didn't, but you wouldn't be in this financial position if he hadn't made you all those empty promises. The least he can do is pay your bills. I told him that too."

Justin groaned. "Mom..."

"Don't 'mom' me. Just listen. I had a long talk with Von. He's just a person—like everyone. He makes mistakes the same as everyone else on the planet. First off, he didn't know about your diagnosis."

"That's because I didn't want him to know. Nobody wants someone to stay with them out of pity."

"Secondly," Kate said over the top of Justin, as if he wasn't speaking. "He knows what he did was wrong, but that boy loves you. Let him make things right. I taught you to forgive people. Not to mention, anything worth having is worth fighting for."

"I hate that saying," Justin growled before he could stop.

"For real. That saying makes people believe they should fight for what they want, even if the battle is killing them. Every time I've put up with some bullshit from Von, I've thought, surely if I've fought this long and hard to be with him, then we must be meant to be. But what I've learned is —that saying is a crock of shit. In truth, I think I've had to fight so hard to keep him because fate was trying to tell me I was on the wrong path. Otherwise, he would've fought for me too, right?" Even Justin heard the pain in his voice, but he couldn't mask it. It didn't matter how he felt. They were still over. Von had still left him, no matter the promises he'd made. It was as if they'd been a dream Justin never wanted to wake from. Only Von's clothes, in the drawer he'd claimed to want, proved they'd ever happened at all. Justin wondered if he should burn them. Maybe it would be cleansing.

"There once was a chance I didn't take," Kate said, pulling Justin from his depressing thoughts.

He scrubbed a hand over his face. "Mom, please don't tell the nursing school story again."

"But our lives might've been so different if I'd taken that chance," she argued.

Justin didn't hesitate in his counter. "Or, I might not have been born."

"My point is," Kate said, speaking over him. "For the rest of my life, I'll wonder if we could've had a nicer home, gone on better vacations, or lived somewhere you would've had an easier time if I'd been braver and gone to school. I worry, if you never take a leap of faith, that you'll wake up one day with more regrets than you can count."

"I only have one regret," Justin said, not bothering to hide his animosity, "and that's ever setting eyes on Von Wolf."

Kate sighed. "I'm always on your side, but sometimes you have to forgive people. Not for their sake, but for yours."

"I'm not strong enough to lose him again." Justin heard the confession fall from his lips as if the words came from someone else. He didn't want to be saying them, but he couldn't avoid the truth.

"Are you strong enough to see him end up with someone else?" Kate asked ruthlessly. "Because that's what will eventually happen, you know? His face is always plastered all over the news. The minute he meets someone else, you'll have to watch it happen. You'll have to sit back and accept it could've been you. Can you do that?" His mom had always been the brutally honest type.

"I don't know," Justin answered honestly.

"Then you're not done," Kate said, sounding triumphant. "Until you don't give a damn where he ends up, you're not finished. Next time you see him, I want you to picture him with someone else, and then go with your gut."

Justin rolled his eyes since she couldn't see him. "If you say so."

"I do, and now I want you to send me all your bills."

"No, Mom," Justin said, drawing the line at her demand.

"Justin Edward Marks, send those fucking bills to me or I will make you sorry."

At the use of his full name, Justin blinked. He was certain he hadn't been called by his full name since he was eight. "Uh, yes, ma'am."

"Today," she added. "Scan them and email them to me."

"All right." Justin winced as he agreed, but he had no other choice. She was his mom.

Her tone softened at Justin's agreement. "I love you, baby. Everything will be okay. You'll see."

"I hope so. I love you too."

"Call me tomorrow."

"I will," Justin said, even though she should've known he would. Since his diagnosis, they'd spoken every day. After all, he no longer knew if one day soon would be his last. Giving up on his pity party, Justin pushed from the bed and went in search of food. In truth, he wasn't even hungry, but it wasn't as if he had anything else to do.

Justin opened cabinet doors and slammed them closed again. Nothing appealed to him. Of course, nowadays, everything tasted like ash anyhow. He should just pick something and settle. Ugh. Justin stamped into his shoes and pulled on his usual stocking cap. Fuck it. Even if he had to drive around all night, he wouldn't fucking settle. Justin knew he was being ridiculous. He just didn't care. Wasn't settling what he always did? To hell with that. He ripped open the front door with more force than necessary. Von scrambled to catch himself from where he'd obviously been sitting against the door, waiting.

"What the fuck are you doing?" Justin asked as he stepped out and pulled the door closed behind him.

Von cleared his throat as if he hadn't expected to get caught or Justin had woken him. "I'm being here for you," Von answered, sounding unsure.

"You're also breaking your word," Justin reminded him.

Von shook his head. "I wasn't bothering you."

"You are now," Justin said, pushing past him and headed for his car.

Von was hot on his heels. "Where do you need to go? I'll take you."

"There's no food in my house. I think I'll hit the drive-thru," he tacked on, because he knew Von would hate it.

"I'll drive."

Von's offer had Justin drawing up short. He eyed Von for

a moment. "You want to take me to get food that you think is bad for me?"

"I'm not your dad," Von said with a shrug. "If that's what you want, I'll drive."

It was obvious Von wasn't going away. Even if Justin shot him down, Von would be waiting on Justin's doorstep for him to return. At least, if Von drove, Justin had the option to jump from the car. Von was too big for Justin to push him out. He shoved his keys in his pocket and changed directions, heading for the truck. Von raced ahead and opened the door for him. Justin realized, as Von slid behind the wheel, his non-nap had calmed him. The immediate inferno of anger over seeing Von again had settled into a simmer.

"Where am I headed?"

Justin shrugged. "I didn't have a place in mind. Pick something. If you've spent all day outside my apartment, I'm sure you're hungry too."

Von kept his gaze locked on the road. "Does that mean I'm welcome to eat with you?"

Justin thought it over. In the grand scheme of things, a meal didn't matter. "I suppose."

While Von drove, Justin stared at the man's profile. His mom's words rang through his head. Could he live with Von being with someone else? Rage boiled in Justin's gut. He'd fucking kill him. Justin turned away, choosing to look at the scenery instead. The sky was violet streaked with orange. Any minute now, the sun would disappear, leaving them in darkness as well as silence. He could feel himself weakening. Life wasn't fair. Anger was all he had.

Von's voice broke the silence. "Will you tell me what happened?"

The soft note to Von's heavy accent made the backs of

Justin's eyes sting. When he'd been in the hospital—when he'd needed Von the most, that was the tone he'd craved. It was soothing and tricked him into believing he wasn't alone in this, but he was.

Justin sniffed, fighting back the hot press of tears. He couldn't look at Von. "Um," Justin said, clearing his throat and trying to decide where to start. "I had another clot. This time, it couldn't be explained away by recent surgery. Plus, my white blood cell count was ridiculously high. They put a filter in my abdomen to catch any future clots, but it wasn't a normal thing to happen, you know?"

Out of the corner of his eye, he saw Von nod. "So, it's lung cancer."

Justin startled at Von's words. "How did you know that?" Even as he asked the question, he knew. Von was smarter than everyone else. If he'd been there, he would've hounded the doctors while reassuring Justin. Justin wouldn't have been left with more questions than answers.

Von shrugged. "That's the most likely thing to cause hypercoagulation. Since you've never been a smoker, I'm assuming they suspect Radon exposure."

All Justin could do was stare at Von in disbelief. The man knew every fucking thing about every fucking thing. "I have no idea. They didn't tell me anything other than I have cancer and let's start treating it. I had questions, of course, but they just kept telling me it could've been any number of things."

Von nodded. "Probably Radon exposure. It's more common than you realize. I never thought about it before, but you were raised in the country, drinking well water. Then you grew up and got a job working in a lab that's located underground. If their ventilation wasn't solid, who knows?"

Despite everything, an unexpected smile exploded across Justin's face. "Guess I should've listened to all your long-winded speeches about my unhealthy lifestyle."

Von didn't smile. A lump rose in Justin's throat. The confession sideswiped Justin and escaped without his permission. "I don't know which is worse—the possibility of dying or having lost you. It's pretty much a cruel tie." Without warning, Von pulled to the side of the road. All Justin could do was watch as he jumped from the truck, slamming the door behind him as he went. Justin's door flew open, and he was in Von's arms. The heat rolling off the man's chest warmed Justin's cheek. He didn't pull away or argue. Instead, Justin pressed closer and forced his mind blank. His eyes already burned from the effort it took not to fall apart.

"You're not allowed to die. I won't let you."

"I don't belong to you anymore. You should go back to Phoenix and never think of me again."

Von's hold tightened.

Justin pushed at his chest. "I'm hungry." He swiped at his eyes as he made the claim. Von's touch hurt—way more than Justin could've anticipated. The rest of the ride was made in silence. When Von pulled into the parking lot of a familiar restaurant, Justin considered crying foul. It was the same pizza place they'd gone to on their first date. Justin decided he wouldn't give the man the satisfaction of seeing his pain. Instead, he held his head high and went inside. A long litany of curse words rang through Justin's head as he stepped through the door. The place smelled amazing.

Unlike the last time they were there, Von didn't try bullying his way into Justin's side of the booth. He sat across from Justin and held his stare. Justin almost got up and joined Von on his side just so the man wouldn't look at him anymore.

"Tell me about your treatments."

Justin opened the menu and ignored Von's demand. "Tell me what's happening with the suspension."

Von didn't respond. Instead, the menu disappeared from Justin's hands. Von replaced it with his phone. "I've been texting you about it."

Justin dropped his gaze to the device in his hands. It was open to a line of unanswered texts. "I blocked you five seconds after you dumped me."

"I suspected as much," Von said, sounding bland.

Rather than reading too much into his words, Justin scrolled back to the first unanswered message and read.

Von: *I'm sorry.*

&

Von: *I miss you.*

&

Von: *Fuck, Justin. I wish you'd answer me so I can take it all back.*

&

Von: *So I guess you're really done with me this time. I know you probably don't care, but I love you.*

Justin rubbed his chest, wishing he didn't have to do this.

&

VON: *I was released from the team today, even though the league hasn't ruled on my case yet. Per my contract, if I get into any trouble in the first two years, I can be released without penalty. Since I know I haven't done anything wrong, I've decided to sue. Damn, what a mess my life has become. I know this bullshit is what I spared you from, but—at the same time—I also recognize I should've never let you go. Fuck, Justin. I never know what the right thing is. Before you, I'd never loved anyone. I don't know why I fuck up everything I touch. The harder I try to keep from hurting you, the more damage I do. You're right to hate me. It's good you ignore me. I'm not worth anyone's time.*

Justin looked up. "You were released? Why would they do that?"

"It wasn't personal," Von said, sounding unconcerned. "They had a lot of money tied up in me and no permanent forward. Letting me go freed up the money they needed to find someone to take my place. In short, it was cheaper to fight a lawsuit than pay me for nothing."

Tearing his gaze away from the blue of Von's eyes that he enjoyed too much, Justin went back to reading.

VON: *Since you never respond to any of my texts, I'm guessing you have me blocked, or you hate me, or both. I don't blame you. This is the only outlet I have, so I keep texting, needing to tell you I love you. The day I said you shouldn't move here, I broke three bones in my hand after putting my fist through the wall. I can admit that here because I don't think you'll ever see it. Justin, I don't know how to love you the way you deserve. No one has ever shown me how. To my father, I was a lifelong science project. I had no friends or family who loved me or needed my love. From*

birth, I was taught nothing mattered more than greatness and achieving goals. The best way I know how to love you is by not publicly embarrassing you. Right now, it's not setting well in my gut. Tell me how to love you. I feel like you were my greatest achievement. At the same time, I must be your biggest letdown. Show me how to fix it.

For a moment, Justin stared at the messages and read them again twice. He swallowed, trying to make the permanent lump in his throat go away. "Did the league ever rule on your case?" Justin asked with his gaze still locked on the phone.

"They ruled there wasn't enough evidence to support the claim of any wrongdoing on my part."

"Will Phoenix hire you back now?" Justin didn't know why he still couldn't look at Von, but he couldn't.

"No."

Justin looked up then. "Why? Is it because they gave your spot away?"

Von shook his head. "Instead of dragging out a long court battle, I settled out of court. As part of the settlement, I retired."

Shock rendered Justin speechless. When he found his voice, Justin sounded every bit as surprised as he felt. "Why? You love hockey. It's not what you do, it's a part of who you are. Why would you retire and leave it behind?"

With a sigh, Von leaned forward and set his elbows on the table. His gaze never left Justin's and Justin couldn't look away. "Hockey left me behind after the suspension. The games came and went each week without me there. Teams won and lost. I didn't even check the scores. After a while, I realized most of my anger was righteous indignation. I knew I hadn't been under contract or signed with any team when

I met that ref. Nothing sucks worse than getting punished and humiliated for something you didn't do. But I made another discovery. Hockey isn't my greatest love. You are."

"Are you ready to order?"

Justin tore his gaze away and focused on the red-haired waitress. "Um, yeah. We'll have the manager's special with two waters. He wants lemon, but I don't."

"You got it," she said, walking away. Too late, Justin realized he should've dragged out giving their order a little longer. Without the waitress there, Justin had nothing to focus on for longer than five seconds at a time. It was always only a matter of time before his gaze slid back to Von. He didn't think Von ever looked away from him.

"You've lost your eyelashes," Von said out of the blue. "I take it you're doing chemo."

Well, wasn't this fucking fantastic? Not only did he already feel subconscious about the way he looked, now Von felt the need to point it out. Justin tapped his fingers on the table and stared at the wall over Von's shoulder. "I've already lost most of my hair. Thanks for noticing."

"You're stunning."

The temptation to roll his eyes was real.

"Two waters. One with the lemon," the waitress said, reappearing and setting their drinks on the table. "Can I get you anything else while you're waiting?" Justin smiled and shook his head. She was off again, leaving them alone.

Von stood, grabbed his water, and shoved Justin over on the bench. His heart cried out in denial as Von's large frame crowded his space. Justin's traitorous body let out a little hum. Von was so warm. Justin was always cold nowadays.

"You still have my phone."

Justin glanced down in surprise. It was Von's phone he

twirled in his hands, needing something to keep him busy. "Sorry." Justin passed it over. Von's hand engulfed Justin's, phone and all. He held on, forcing Justin to meet his stare.

"Your hands are cold."

Something black rose inside Justin. "Is my nose red too? Maybe you'd like to point out the dark circles under my eyes. You have me trapped here, so now's the time for you to log all your complaints about my current state."

Instead of getting sucked into Justin's bitterness, Von set his phone aside and threw his arm over Justin's shoulders. He tucked Justin closer once again, making Justin's stupid body happier than it had been in ages. "It's funny, you know?"

Justin seriously considered punching him. "Now I'm funny to you. This keeps getting better by the minute."

A low chuckle slipped from Von. The sound hit Justin in the chest. "That's not what I meant, and you know it. What I meant is—it's funny how when we're apart, I question if I can love you the way you deserve." Von's gaze dropped to Justin's mouth. "When we're together, I know no one else could possibly love you more than I do."

"Here you go, guys—one manager's special. A large vegetarian thin crust. Can I get you anything else?"

"And you still love me," Von said, ignoring the waitress.

Justin couldn't tear his gaze away from Von's intense stare. The texts he'd read on Von's phone wouldn't leave his brain or heart in peace. Von had begged for forgiveness. It wasn't like he'd waited either. He'd wanted to take his words back immediately, but Justin had him blocked. It didn't matter. Justin hurt. It fucking mattered because Justin hurt. "No."

"I'll come back," the waitress said, sounding uncomfortable.

"You don't like vegetarian pizza. Only I do. Yet this is what you ordered. You might be angry. Hell, you should be, but you still put me ahead of yourself. You still love me."

Justin's vision dimmed around the edges. Each breath came harder than the last. He hated these moments. The stress of Von was too much for Justin's weak body, but he couldn't stop arguing. "I'm not hungry and I don't love you." Unfortunately, Justin panted the words as he struggled for oxygen, taking away the power from his claim. Justin snapped his teeth together and sucked air. God, he hated this. He fucking hated Von.

PANIC SQUEEZED at Von's heart. Justin's face had gone pale. He wheezed with every breath. He was certain Justin hadn't noticed the way he'd surrendered more of his weight to Von until Von was practically the only thing keeping him upright in the booth.

Von cast a desperate look around. He spotted the waitress and waved her over. "Could you box this up and bring me the check?"

Her gaze slid Justin's way. A hint of worry crossed her features, but she didn't let her cheerful tone slip. "Sure." Von appreciated her not pointing out Justin's state. He doubly appreciated the way she rushed through getting them out of there, and he showed it by leaving her a huge tip. Von carried the pizza in one hand while keeping Justin upright with one arm around his waist. The fact that Justin didn't argue said more than the man's harsh breathing. After helping him into the truck, Von buckled the man's seat belt for him. The ride back to Justin's apartment was made in silence with the exception of every breath Justin struggled to draw. Those were ragged and rapid. Von felt more helpless by the minute. He couldn't decide if he needed to take Justin home or the hospital. By the time they made it to Justin's place, Justin had leaned his head back and closed his eyes. Von didn't think he was sleeping.

"Hand me your keys and I'll unlock the door first."

Proving Von had been right about him not sleeping, Justin dug his keys from his pocket and passed them Von's way. Von unlocked the door, tossed the pizza inside, and went back for Justin. Rather than allowing Justin to lean on him, Von swept the man into his arms and carried him inside. Justin still didn't argue. Von thought he'd known real fear before now. He thought he'd been scared of losing Justin before. There was no comparison. Von ground his back teeth to stop them from chattering. It wasn't hard for Von to find Justin's room in the one-bedroom apartment. He kept his eyes locked on his path—straight to Justin's bed—to keep from losing his shit. Von wasn't strong in the ways that mattered. He couldn't survive knowing Justin wasn't in the world somewhere—alive and happy. He wasn't strong enough to be left behind.

"Still hate you," Justin said as Von pulled off his shoes and tucked him into bed.

He kept his gaze locked on his task. "You should."

"I believed in you."

A lump rose in Von's throat.

"I needed you," Justin said so low Von barely heard.

Von's eyes burned from the hot press of tears. "You deserved better. I will be better. Now, tell me how I can help." The low, raspy tint to Von's voice was out of his control. He hurt more than he ever thought possible.

Justin's eyes were closed. His chest expanded as if he was

concentrating on his breathing. "There's a bag on the kitchen table. It looks like a backpack. My oxygen is inside."

Von didn't need to hear more. He was off, easily finding the machine and returning to Justin's side. Without asking for Justin's permission, he put the mask on Justin's face. Justin didn't budge or complain. Terror had Von checking Justin's pulse. It was steady. Either he'd passed out or had fallen asleep. While sucking air, Von bent at the waist and set his forehead on Justin's chest. If he'd ever been more scared in his life, he couldn't remember it. He didn't have the strength to leave Justin alone. In fact, if Justin wanted him gone, he'd have to call the police to pry him out of there, because Von couldn't do it.

Once he had his breathing under control, Von walked through the house. After finding a spot in the fridge for the pizza, he checked the locks and turned out the lights before returning to Justin's side. He peeled off the man's socks. Von knew how much Justin hated sleeping in them. Next, he rearranged the pillows, making a spot for Justin's oxygen where it wouldn't move. Once he had everything arranged just right, he ensured the covers were tucked around Justin's body before kicking off his shoes and crawling in beside Justin.

For the longest time, he simply listened to Justin breathing. He'd missed the feeling of having Justin sleeping beside him. Being without this man had been like missing a limb. The time he'd spent fighting his suspension seemed so petty and useless. He'd stuck to his workout routine and private ice sessions, expecting he'd rejoin the season at any moment. He'd fought, thinking the sooner he had shit together, the sooner he could fix things with Justin. Von could've flown back and tried winning Justin back sooner, but his attention would've been split between issues. Justin deserved to have his undivided attention. Now Justin had it, whether he wanted it or not. Von would stop at nothing to win this man. Maybe he hadn't always been good at proving it, but Justin was the greatest love of Von's life. No way in hell would Justin ever get rid of him. Even Justin's hatred was better than nothing at all.

9

*T*here was something heavy across his legs, pinning him to the bed. Justin's eyes shot open. A large chest blocked his line of sight. Memories of the night before overcame Justin. He'd lost track of time. Fifteen minutes or fifteen hours could've passed for all he knew. His alarm clock hadn't gone off, so he must not be late for work yet. Von was so freaking huge and warm, Justin felt like he was in a cocoon. Reality didn't reach him with Von holding him. Without thought, Justin scooched closer. His oxygen mask kept him from sniffing Von's skin. Justin shoved it out of the way before burying his face against Von's chest.

Von's deep breaths let Justin know the man slept peacefully through Justin nosing up his chest, seeking any hint of the man's subtle cologne. He found it near Von's collarbone. A clean, flowery scent filled Justin's nostrils. He couldn't stop inhaling it. Dark thoughts rose to the surface, but Justin stamped them down. Too few good things happened to Justin any longer. He wasn't above stealing a moment no one would know about but him. Justin's lies still rang in his head. He'd told Von he didn't love him anymore. As if his love could die. If Justin knew how to kill it, he would, but this fucking spot—the place right below Von's collarbone—Justin wanted to lick it. Temptation crippled him. He couldn't move away.

The delicious flavor of Von's skin exploded across Justin's tongue, making him realize how far he'd gone. His mouth was open and sucking on the man's chest without a single thought. Horror crawled up Justin's spine, making goosebumps form on his skin. Justin didn't stop. He felt Von stop breathing. The man's muscles tensed, as if he was afraid to move an inch. Justin bit back a smile at the thought of rendering Von helpless. In the past, this was all it would take for Von to be hard for him. The desire to check was a real thing.

It suddenly hit Justin—he didn't know why he held back. Life was so fucking short. Did it really matter if he touched Von? Since his diagnosis, he'd found he regretted the things he hadn't done more than the things he had. Von had already broken him beyond all repair. There was no more damage the man could do. Before even Justin had accepted his decision, Justin shaped Von's erection through his jeans. With his eyes closed, Justin could pretend things were different. He could block out the rage he felt each time he set eyes on Von. It had been four months since Von left for Phoenix. It had been sixteen long weeks since anyone had touched him. Damn, he'd missed the sensation of Von's hard body beneath his palms. Chances were better than not he'd beat this cancer, but what if he didn't? Did he want to spend what was left of his life never having anyone touch him? He could use Von for sex and not get hurt. Justin already hurt.

Von tilted his chin back, giving Justin better access to kiss his neck. He cupped the back of Justin's head, holding him in place. Moving slowly, Justin slid Von's zipper down before working the man's button loose. The front of Von's underwear was already wet. As Von's erection filled Justin's hand, doubts crept in. How many men had Von fucked since he left? Without any plan in place, Justin's mouth moved back to Von's chest, and the question slipped out.

"How many men took my place once you decided you were done with me?"

"I haven't slept with anyone else since you tripped over me in the freezer section." The words came out sounding harsh. Von was such a liar. Everything he said was suspect. A fresh wave of pain and regret washed over Justin. Funny how it didn't dampen his lust. His cock begged to be set free. Rather than questioning Von's claim, Justin stroked Von's erection. With every slide of soft skin against Justin's palm, his heartache grew. It didn't make sense why he couldn't separate himself from the experience. His alarm clock blared to life, giving Justin the excuse he needed to roll out of Von's hold. After switching off the alarm, Justin slowly sat up to keep from throwing his breathing out of sync by moving too fast. He set his feet on the floor and stared at nothing. Justin's body hated him. His heart hated him even more.

"Justin—"

"I have to go to work," Justin said, moving away and heading for the bathroom. He stared at his reflection as he brushed his teeth. At some point in the night, he'd lost his stocking cap. He looked a mess, and Von had seen it all. Justin tried not to think. The worst of his usual dark thoughts were trying to push their way in. He didn't have the willpower he needed today. He had no desire to convince himself to keep fighting—to keep living. Justin tore his gaze away from his reflection. He couldn't look at himself any longer.

After turning the water as hot as it would go, Justin stepped beneath the steaming stream. His skin turned red, yet Justin still shook from the inside out. When he'd started chemo, his doctor had suggested Justin join a support group as well. The man had warned Justin that he would have days like this—days when his mind would whisper he should just give up. There was nothing for him here. He was tired. Battle weary. Broken. The tickle at the back of his throat warned him that the water running down his face wasn't all from the shower. Justin dipped his head beneath the stream of water, hoping to wash away any tears that might be mixing in.

Cool air slapped his skin as Von ripped back the shower curtain. Justin could only stare at him in silence. Damn, he'd forgotten how fucking beautiful Von was without clothes. Before he had time to choose a reaction, Von's nude body pressed against his. Von's mouth covered Justin's, cutting off any chance of an argument. Justin's back was against the wall and his legs were around Von's waist before he knew what was happening. By then, he no longer cared. The strong stroke of Von's tongue gave Justin strength. He'd been weak for so fucking long. Allowing Von's kiss didn't feel weak, as he would've expected. Instead, it felt the way it always had—like he was the most powerful person in the world in that moment.

The head of Von's cock pressed against Justin's asshole. Von ripped his mouth away and held Justin's stare as he pressed inside. "Be angry," Von said, taking Justin by surprise and confusing him, considering what the man did to Justin's body. "Fight me and tell me you hate me," he added, leaving Justin torn between crying out in pleasure and just plain crying. Von leaned his weight against Justin and changed angles, pulling a moan from Justin. "It doesn't matter if you believe me when I say I love you, because I do fucking love you. Yell. Scream. Try to throw me out." Von's tone softened as he leaned closer, pumping inside Justin. "Just don't give up, okay?" He didn't give Justin a chance to respond. His lips lightly touched Justin's, stealing his thoughts.

Justin's fingers dug into Von's shoulders and tugged at his hair. He tried touching as many places as he could reach. His body was on fire, ready to explode, and Von hadn't even touched his dick. Incapable of standing another second of his cock aching, Justin palmed his erection. It was a mindless act. Von growled against Justin's mouth, sounding more turned on than any man should. The noises the man made had Justin's balls drawing up tight.

"Goddamn, baby. I love you."

At Von's claim, Justin's traitorous body betrayed him. An orgasm slammed into him with a force he hadn't experienced in a long time. It rocked Justin to his core. Gasps tore from his throat. Struggling for air had become a familiar experience for him, but this was different. There were no other phenomena on the planet that matched the way Von stole his breath.

Von threw his head back and sucked air. The cords in his neck stood out as he came. He cried Justin's name. Justin couldn't look away. His eyes burned from the effort it took for him not to blink. The way Von's hard body became even more solid during orgasm always fascinated Justin. There was no one more beautiful than this man who easily balanced Justin's weight and controlled their every move. He didn't think anyone in their right mind would blame him for being weak. One glance at Von would rob anyone of their good sense.

When Von's chin dropped and their gazes collided, Justin stopped breathing. There was so much emotion swimming in the man's eyes. Justin didn't really exist when Von wasn't around. He went through the motions of living, but he was a shadow of himself. Justin was only whole when Von held him. It was beyond cruel. Von allowed Justin's feet to slide to the floor, but he didn't release Justin. Instead, he grabbed the body wash and set to gently washing Justin's skin. Justin couldn't fight. All his concentration was on his next breath.

"I've missed doing this for you," Von said, sounding every bit as wrecked as Justin felt.

An unexpected burst of anger ran through Justin's blood. Von wouldn't have missed a goddamn thing if he hadn't run for the hills and deemed Justin too much of a burden. He could've been in the shower with Justin every fucking day if he hadn't dumped Justin. As a matter of fact, he could've come back at any fucking time in the past few months and tried to fix things. Instead, he'd been too goddamn worried about his career. Justin swallowed, trying to keep from flying into a rage.

"I have to go to work," Justin said, shoving his way past Von and grabbing a towel. Without looking back, he dried his skin as he headed for the bedroom. He had to get the hell out of there. Justin should've known better than to think Von would let him run away. He was hot on Justin's trail.

"There's no reason to feel guilty, Justin. You aren't weak. We've always been explosive together and your heart knows where you belong."

Justin somehow kept his tone bland as he threw on the

first clothes he found. "I don't feel guilty. You of all people should know I never do anything I don't want to do. Plus, it was just sex."

"Okay, ouch," Von drawled.

Justin tried not to rub the spot in his chest that ached over Von's reaction. It was stupid, so fucking ridiculous that he cared he'd hurt Von with his words. He'd be goddamned before he took them back. He weaved a belt through his belt loops and tried not to think about it.

"I'm running late to work."

Von grabbed some clothes from his drawer, the one Justin had been too weak to empty, even after moving. For a moment, Von blinked in surprise at his clothes—like he'd grabbed them out of habit before realizing what he'd done. He eyed the dresser before turning Justin's way. Justin looked away, refusing to meet the man's gaze. Von pulled his clothes on, obviously deciding to say nothing of the incident. Instead, he picked another argument that pissed off Justin.

"It's ridiculous for you to go to work now that I'm here."

"You should go home, Von," Justin said, hoping he wouldn't rip the man's head from his body only minutes after he'd given Justin such an explosive orgasm.

Von stretched a T-shirt over his massive chest and tugged it down his torso, covering his gorgeous abs. "I don't have a home. The moment I finished signing the papers to settle out of court with Luka, I hit the road to come back to you."

"I'm sure you'll land on your feet," Justin said, sounding like an asshole and not caring.

"Justin, I've got you covered. Now's the time for you to relax and worry about getting better. Fuck working. Just call and let them know you're done. I'll take care of you. Let me do this. Get back in bed and I'll baby you until this is all a bad memory."

It was such a shot to the gut. Every word leaving Von's was like a twist of a knife. At one time, he would've given anything to hear those words from Von. It was too little too late.

§

JUSTIN'S SHIRT clung to his skin in the places where he hadn't fully dried before pulling on the material. The sight was distracting Von. His need to take care of Justin was making him half crazed. Like a mother hen, he wanted to rip the shirt from the man's back and dress him in something dry so he wouldn't catch his death the moment he stepped outside. Unfortunately, Justin kept opening his mouth and infuriating Von.

"I gave up my job for you once, Von. Remember how that turned out? I can't afford to take another chance on you. You've proven way too many times you can't be trusted."

The anger simmering in Von's gut wouldn't cool, but he refused to give in to the explosion. Justin needed him whether he admitted it or not. This was too important for him to back down. After seeing Justin last night, barely breathing, Von couldn't lose this argument. "If you won't quit, then I suggest you pick which job you like or the one that wears you out the least, because you're not working two. My accountant is already in the process of taking care of your medical bills. You don't have to worry over them any longer. If you want to keep one job to prove a point to me or make yourself feel better, that's fine. But I won't sit back and quietly watch you kill yourself to spite me." Despite his best efforts, each word had come out as if growled through his teeth. Justin didn't look concerned.

"Fine," Justin said, pulling on a flannel shirt over his T-shirt.

Von's eyebrows snapped together. "That's it? Just fine?"

Justin sat down and held Von's stare. "You're not forgiven."

"That's fair."

Justin ignored Von's interruption. "We're not back together. The only reason you're still here is because I'm not stupid enough to think I can make you leave and I don't have the energy to try. If you need to stay here to ease your guilty conscience or whatever, then fine, but don't think I don't see through you. The first time you get a better offer, whether it be hockey or another man, you'll be gone." Justin tied his shoes as if he wasn't ripping out Von's heart.

Von breathed through the pain of Justin no longer believing in him. "There's no such thing as a better offer than you."

Justin shrugged. It couldn't have been more apparent he didn't believe a word Von said. "It doesn't matter. There's nothing left of my heart for you to break." Justin stood. "Have a good day doing whatever it is you do. There's a spare key hanging on the key hook in the kitchen, in case you need to go somewhere. Just please don't bring another man to my apartment."

The pain of Justin's indifference clawed at Von's insides. He stood. "Let me drive you to work. I'd rather you didn't drive after last night's episode."

Justin eyed him—emotionless. "If that's what you want."

"It is," Von said as he headed for his shoes. He needed to know where Justin was at all times and the man couldn't run away. This wouldn't be an overnight fix. He needed time and to know Justin was okay. Unfortunately, Von couldn't ignore the tiny voice in the back of his mind that grew stronger every day. The one telling him he'd gone too far this time. Justin would never love him the same way again.

The ride to Justin's work was a nightmare. Justin didn't talk to him other than ensuring Von didn't get lost on the way. The new lab where Justin put his degree to work was smaller than the last. Most likely, it paid less as well. Another black mark against Von. The moment they arrived, Justin jumped from the truck, stealing any chance Von had of trying to kiss him goodbye. Before Von backed from the parking space, his phone buzzed.

Justin: *I forgot to tell you I get off at 5:30.*

Von: *Hey, I'm unblocked. Does that mean I get to send nudes?*

Justin didn't respond. Von wasn't surprised. Since he had to pick his battles, Von pulled away from the building, leaving Justin behind. He had a million and one things to do before five thirty rolled around. He was about to bowl Justin over, but first, he needed all the info he could get and there was only one person he could go to who still seemed to be somewhat on his side. At the first red light he came to, Von dialed Kate's number.

Kate didn't bother saying hello. "Justin didn't appreciate learning I'd talked to you."

Von had figured as much. "I know, but I wanted to let you know I've sent all the bills to my accountant. They'll be taken care of." His claim was met with silence.

Finally, Kate released a sigh. "You really do love my son, don't you?"

"Yes."

"Then you're just an idiot."

Von swallowed a laugh. "Yes."

"Has he budged a single inch or are you still sitting outside his apartment?"

"He's letting me stay with him, but it's not because he's budged," Von admitted.

Another silence filled the line before Kate responded so quietly he had to strain to hear. "I'm glad he's not alone." Kate blew out another sigh as if every word she spoke went against her best judgment. "I'm afraid for him."

Fear tightened Von's chest. "He won't talk to me about his treatment."

"I'm not worried over that. My son will beat this, but he's not the same."

He'd noticed, but Kate knew more than Von did. Von needed every detail. "How so?"

"This isn't to make you feel bad," Kate said, letting Von know he was at fault. "But Justin had a good job he was proud of and is used to having a steady life. He did as he pleased before you left and he got sick. Justin has always been independent and loved exercising as well as the outdoors. Now, he's working at a job he hates because they let him have the time off he needs. He's missing part of a lung and needs oxygen to get by."

Goddamn. It was worse than he thought.

"Even when the chemo is done, his life will never be the same." Kate took a breath, sounding on the verge of tears. "He's grown quiet, and I can feel him hurting, but he won't talk about it. It's like I'm watching him slip further away by the day. I'm glad you're there."

"I won't let him slip away," Von promised, meaning it from the bottom of his soul.

"For once, I hope you're telling the truth, because people can die of a broken heart. I can't lose my son, but he's lost too many pieces of himself in too short of a period of time, and I don't know if anyone can fix this."

The lump living in Von's throat nearly choked him at Kate's confession. "Don't worry. I retired just so I could dog his heels and make him love me."

A light chuckle caressed Von's ear. "Oh, he loves you. Loving you was never the problem."

Von hoped Kate was right. Justin wasn't the only one who could die from a broken heart.

JUSTIN'S HEART was at odds with his mind like never before. Logically, he knew staying indifferent to Von was the right and smart move. That knowledge didn't stop the giddiness from rising inside him as he left work to find Von waiting. The instant Justin stepped out the door, Von slid from the truck and opened the passenger side door for him. The amount of concentration it took for Justin not to smile like an idiot was off the charts. He knew everyone inside had their faces pressed to the window. Tomorrow, he'd get peppered with questions. Justin didn't know how to answer them. The one thing he did know was there'd be some sighing and jealous bitches at his workplace.

As usual, Von leaned across Justin and buckled his seat belt. It never occurred to him to argue he wasn't helpless. Justin knew that wasn't why Von did the things he did. The man was a lion at heart. A protector. Von's lips brushed his. The kiss was over as it quickly as it began. Their gazes met for a moment before Von closed the door. Justin dropped his chin and gave in to a quick smile while Von wasn't there to witness it. He rearranged his features as Von slipped behind the wheel.

"I brought your oxygen in case you need it."

Justin glanced over, catching sight of the black backpack. "Thank you. I sit all day, so I'm usually fine at work, but I do need to stop and get some groceries, so I might need it."

"I got groceries while you were working," Von said, backing out of the parking space. He flashed a quick smile Justin's way as he shifted into drive. "Don't worry. I know what you like."

"I wasn't worried," Justin said. He wasn't. As much as Von always complained and lectured when it came to Justin's eating habits, he never tried to stop Justin from doing as he pleased.

"How was your day?" Von asked as he turned right from the parking lot, heading for Justin's apartment.

Justin shrugged, even though Von wasn't looking at him. "It was a day. I worked. How was yours?"

"Productive. I cleaned, shopped, arranged to have my things moved from Phoenix, and talked to your mama."

Justin knew Von had deliberately named things in that order. He'd piqued Justin's curiosity over where Von intended to move his things to and then spun Justin in a new direction by chatting with his mom. Justin didn't respond as he tried gathering his thoughts and forming a reaction. His mom was Von's biggest cheerleader, but he knew—if push came to shove—she'd tear Von to shreds. Taking a moment to think ended up saving Justin from over-reacting.

"What did you learn from Mom?"

"Not much. Mostly, we talked about your papa's dialysis. I gave her some suggestions to share with his doctor. Your healthcare system is such shit here. I think they care more about the money than patient care."

"I wish you'd been here for me," Justin said without

thought. With a wince, he scrambled to explain. "That came out wrong. I meant that several times I thought you'd understand what the doctors offered better than I do, and I would've felt better prepared to make the right decisions."

Von nodded. "I think you said what you meant the first time, and you're right. I should've been here. It'll either anger you or relieve you that I did look over the procedures you've been billed for to get an idea of the treatments and prognosis." He tossed a quick glance Justin's way. "You made the only choices you could for the best outcome possible. This is a horrible thing, and it's not fair. In fact, it enrages me because it couldn't have happened to a less deserving person, but you're also the strongest person I know. When this is over, and it will be over, no one will ever know anything happened, because I know you. You'll find a way to be who you were before this awful thing took hold. You're too stubborn for it to be otherwise."

And damned if that wasn't the speech he'd needed to hear from the moment he'd gotten sick. Instead, everyone told him to keep his chin up or do yoga. In fact, he'd heard every condescending and placating bunch of bullshit a person could hear. Before Justin could think of a way to respond, Von found more to say.

"Also, this isn't who you are. This is just something happening to you. It doesn't change what makes you so amazing—like your delicious intelligence and gorgeous smile. The way your eyes flash when a perverted thought crosses your mind." Von reached down and adjusted his jeans as if the thought alone turned him on. Justin hadn't felt the least bit sexy in months. In a matter of a few well-placed words, Von gave it back to him. "I could go on all day, but I need to drive and get us home safely."

It was getting harder not to smile. Justin concentrated on

keeping his face blank for the remainder of the ride. As soon as they were home, Justin went straight for the kitchen. All his lack of eating for the past two days was catching up to him. In fact, he was hungrier than he'd been in a long time. He opened his cabinets, seeing several meals he'd loved to have.

"What do you want for dinner?" Justin asked as he eyed the contents of the fridge.

Von's arms encircled his waist, drawing Justin back against his solid body. Justin's dick immediately stirred. "I want you to do whatever you need to do while I make dinner." His lips brushed Justin's shoulder, nearly causing Justin to pant. "Take a shower. Put on something comfortable. Relax. I've got you."

Justin didn't know how he was supposed to relax with Von touching him and kissing his shoulder. Still, he stepped away from the fridge, determined to do just that. "If you insist." Before he could get away, Von held tight, capturing his attention. When their gazes met, Justin knew what would happen next. He could pull away, deny Von's kiss. His feet wouldn't budge.

"I've always like spoiling you," Von said before touching his lips to Justin's. Justin's heart slowed before racing. Von always stole his breath with every stroke of his tongue. Unfortunately, the man also stole everything else as well and he might like spoiling Justin, but only in short bursts, before he found something better to do.

10

They fell into an odd routine. Von didn't leave. Justin never asked him to either. At some point, it became a habit for Von to take him everywhere and take care of everything. More and more of his things invaded Justin's apartment each day. Justin didn't mention it. Not that he knew what to say anyhow. Von never missed an opportunity to touch or kiss Justin unless they were in bed. Once they were under the covers, it was up to Justin to initiate anything sexual. If Justin didn't start things, it didn't happen. He hadn't decided how he felt about that. Sometimes he thought Von was playing games with him, because Justin found himself going to outrageous lengths to see if Von would break, but he never did. If Justin wanted sex, he had to start it. Justin was by no means starved for affection. Von held him, talked to him nonstop, and never left his side. Justin still couldn't take that leap and say they were a couple because they weren't. Von had proven one too many times he didn't want a real relationship. He just liked playing the part until something else snagged his attention.

Justin stared at his reflection as he dressed. Under Von's

care, he'd regained some of the weight he'd lost. Before Von moved in, if Justin didn't feel good, he didn't eat. Von never let that mess go on, even if it meant spoon-feeding him. He hadn't figured out why Von stayed. Mostly, Justin didn't let himself think about it too much.

Justin's cellphone buzzed across the bathroom counter, snagging his attention. He opened his messages. They poured in like a flood. A smile exploded across Justin's face. He burst from the bathroom, going in search of Von. He found him in the kitchen.

"Look what Jamie just sent me." Justin moved in close, and Von shifted in behind him, putting his arms around Justin's waist and staring at the phone over Justin's shoulder.

Jamie: *I'm sorry we had to skip town without saying good-bye. Our surrogate, Bethany, went into labor early. Meet our daughter, Luna Arbor Roussel.*

Dozens of pictures followed. Luna was pink and tiny. Her eyes were wide open and green like Hawke's.

"Oh my God," Justin breathed. "Jamie wasn't lying. He'll have to kill a fuckboi someday."

"She's beautiful," Von said over Justin's shoulder, almost sounding sad.

Justin glanced over. "Are you okay?"

Von's arms tightened on Justin's waist. A smile stretched his lips. It looked forced and brittle. He nodded toward the phone. "Is this something you'd want for yourself? I never thought to ask what you dreamed of having most from life."

With a shrug, Justin closed the messages. "I guess I never really thought about it, since I don't have their life."

"What do you mean you don't have 'their' life?"

Justin stepped out of Von's hold. He kept his gaze averted as he answered. "They're loyal to each other, putting each other above all others." Justin shrugged again. "I don't know. They're happy."

"And you're not. I see."

At Von's dead tone, Justin's head snapped up. He tried meeting the man's stare, but Von wouldn't look at him.

"Are you ready? Your chemo is in half an hour."

Guilt twisted Justin's gut. He couldn't claim he hadn't known he was hurting Von by not giving him all of himself. Today was the first time he'd not liked himself for it. He made several attempts to cheer up Von on the way to his appointment. It was useless. Von stared into space, lost in his thoughts. Justin worried at his bottom lip and scolded himself. Why was he doing this? At some point, had he become a child over this entire matter? Did he even know what he hoped to accomplish? He hadn't sent Von away nor did he have any intention of doing so. Maybe Justin had thought—in the beginning—that he was protecting his heart, but the truth was—he'd done no such thing. If he eventually succeeded at driving Von away, it would crush him. There'd be no one to blame but himself. There was a very real possibility that Von would skip out him again. Justin couldn't control what Von did, but he could control the way he treated the man. For a moment, he stared at the IV dripping meds that would make him feel like death for two days. When he'd first started these treatments, he'd done them alone—steeped in misery. Now they were so much easier, because Von was there.

Reaching over, he stroked the top of Von's hand until the man turned it palm up so Justin could link fingers with him. It was such a tiny thing, having someone hold his hand, but there was nothing small about it at all, really. Having someone to cling to was a huge anchor, keeping him from drifting away.

"I never really thought about having kids," Justin said without looking at Von, but he clung tight. He couldn't let Von slip away. "In a way, I guess I thought that wasn't some-thing in the cards for me." Justin snorted. "On the other hand, I did think I'd travel the world someday, so I guess I've never been smart about what options are open for me."

"I don't have a dream," Von surprised him by confessing.

Justin chuckled. "I should suppose not. Your dreams have all come true. Not many people can say they've accom-plished what you have."

Von's grip tightened on Justin's hand and his thumb stroked back and forth over Justin's. "I did what my papa wanted. Don't get me wrong, I love playing hockey, but I've never had anything that was for me alone." He brought their joined hands to his lips and nibbled on Justin's knuckles. He stared into space, seeming to think things over, before adding, "Except you, of course. I thought we'd grow old together, doing nothing special other than loving each other —being together."

Justin's heart hurt. He'd done that. He'd put the past tense in Von's speech—was slowly destroying the man's hope.

"That does sound nice," Justin admitted, hoping to make things better. He'd never considered himself a cruel man before now. "I don't guess I've ever pictured myself growing old either, but every dream I've had included you."

Von finally met his gaze. This time, the man's smile was real. It stirred something inside Justin's chest—something Justin thought long dead. Von's smile slipped, but his eyes softened.

"I'm sorry for everything I've done. I'm not sure if I ever said that."

Justin honestly couldn't remember, but Von's words

mattered to Justin's heart. "You've shown it even if you haven't said it."

"I guess I thought we were indestructible."

Justin looked away and nodded. Maybe they were. After all, they might be limping along, but they were still standing together.

§

EACH WEEK, it got a little harder to resist Von. Justin couldn't shake the idea of Von picturing them growing old together. Every day, Justin wanted it too until that dream was all he could think about. Unfortunately, he'd built a wall so tall and strong, even Justin no longer knew how to move past the pain. Von was making it easier with the way he was looking at Justin tonight. Over an hour earlier, he'd grabbed Justin a blanket, pulled Justin into his arms on the couch, and snuggled in. There was no TV or noise whatsoever to distract them. Von still hadn't been the one to initiate sex with Justin since he'd moved in. The way Von was staring at him now had Justin wondering if things were shifting his way. Even though he'd gone to chemo today and felt terrible, Justin worried Von's refusal to make love to him meant they weren't getting better.

Von toyed with Justin's bottom lip while staring at it like a starving man. The scariest thought Justin ever experienced sneaked in. What if Von really stayed this time? What if he meant every promise? Each breath Justin took came harder than the last. He wanted to believe.

Justin couldn't tear his gaze away from Von's face as the man lowered his head. Even as Von captured the lip he'd been playing with, Justin couldn't close his eyes. Von scowled when he kissed. It was one more detail about the man he would've never learned if he hadn't let Von stay. If he let the man get away, how many details would he miss out on learning in the future? He allowed his eyes to slide closed. Justin spent a moment enjoying Von's flavor—like orange and mint. Without warning, the dam in Justin's chest broke. Emotions poured through him until he shook from the power of them.

Von pulled away. Concern etched his features as he stroked Justin's jaw. "What is it?"

"Von, I—"

Someone knocked on the door. As one, they both glanced toward the slab of wood that separated them from the rest of the world. No one ever stopped by. Justin didn't have any friends. His parents lived two states away, and Jamie and Hawke had gone back home to England. With a sigh that sounded a lot like regret, Von slid out from beneath him before tucking the throw blanket around him once more.

"You stay put. I'll take care of it. It's probably someone trying to sell us something or convert us."

Justin swallowed down a happy hum as he watched Von cross the room. He loved the way the man moved. In truth, he loved everything about Von. He just loved him. If they hadn't been interrupted, Justin would've admitted as much. The door opened and Justin's emotions dried up. His heart hardened. Luka Turner stood on the other side.

"Luka," Von said, sounding surprised. He stepped aside, inviting Luka inside. "What brings you... how did you know where to find me?"

A gigantic mocha-skinned male with awesome eyes stepped through the door behind Luka. Justin's money was on the man being Luka's bodyguard. He looked like someone Justin would want watching his back.

Luka motioned toward the man. "You remember my husband, Brady."

"Of course," Von said, shaking the man's hand, even though Brady looked like if he had his way, he'd snap Von in two instead.

Von turned and waved in Justin's direction. "This is Justin. He's mine."

Justin bit the inside of his cheek to keep from smiling at Von's choice of words. Luka turned a kind smile Justin's way, making it hard for Justin to hang on to his animosity toward the man who'd not only dated Justin's man but fired him for no reason.

"It's nice to meet you, Justin. Jamie has told me a lot of great things about you."

"Sang your praises for half an hour, actually," Brady added, surprising Justin with how deep his voice sounded.

Justin's smile grew more genuine by the second. It was hard to hate anyone who was a friend of Jamie's. "Please have a seat," Justin said, struggling to sit up and make room.

Von rushed to his side. "Nope. You stay put," he ordered as he grabbed Justin's legs and sat down. He set Justin's legs in his lap and massaged them. Damn, it felt good. He was so sore all over.

Brady and Luka took the loveseat.

"What brings you by?" Von asked. Despite his steady voice and neutral expression, Justin could feel the tension rolling off the man's body. His discomfort fed Justin's.

Luka leaned forward and set his elbows on his knees as he focused on Von. "I'm sure you heard that Reynolds broke a leg and will be out for the remainder of the season."

Von's hands stilled. Justin didn't know who Reynolds was, but it was apparent Von did. "No," Von said. His voice sounded dead. "I've had more important things to do than follow the season."

Luka nodded. His closed expression never slipped. "I'd like to have you back. At thirty-eight, twenty-five, and eleven, we're third in the western league. These last nine games could make us or break us. We need you. Not only for this year," Luka said, obviously attempting to sweeten his deal.

Von wasn't looking at anyone.

Justin was resigned. Von wouldn't choose to stay. If roles were reversed, Justin wouldn't choose him either. Millions or a man who had more bad days than good—there was no choice, really. Justin tried finding some anger or outrage to cling to, hoping to save himself from the impending heartache. He couldn't find any. Von loved hockey. Justin loved Von. There was nothing to discuss.

"It's okay, Von," Justin said, surprising even himself with the honesty in his voice. It was okay. Justin loved Von enough to set him free. "I know it's what you love."

Von glanced over and smiled. A lump rose in Justin's throat. He'd miss this man for the rest of his life, but Von deserved happiness too. "No," Von said, still smiling. "This is what I love, being here with you." His gaze moved back to Luka, leaving Justin shocked speechless. "Thank you for the offer, but I'll have to pass."

Luka shook his head. "If this is about what happened at the beginning of the season—"

Von made a slashing motion, cutting Luka off. "Not at all. As I told you before I left town, there're no hard feelings. Hockey is a business for us. This isn't about that. I'm done. All I want is to drive Justin crazy with my constant presence until he begs me to find something else to do."

Before Luka could respond, Justin butted in. "I'm afraid this is my fault. You see, I've been battling cancer for several months." Justin pulled his stocking cap down lower, feeling self-conscious as he made the confession. "Von doesn't want to leave me alone. Do you mind giving us a few minutes alone so we can discuss it?" Justin tried moving from the couch, determined to take things to the bedroom.

Luka stood. "We'll step outside so you don't have to get up."

Justin flashed him a grateful smile. "You don't have to do that, but I appreciate it." Some people breezed through chemo. Justin thanked every deity listening that he only had two treatments left. They kicked his ass every single time. He'd hated the thought of moving from the couch. Luka and Brady stood and headed for the door, leaving Justin to relax. The moment the door closed behind them, Justin pounced. "You can't give up hockey for me. Not only would I never ask that of you, I'll never be able to live with myself if you're sitting around here miserable instead of winning another championship."

One corner of Von's mouth lifted, as if he found Justin's claims ridiculous. "I don't want another championship. It means nothing."

Exasperation rose inside Justin. "Von, I love you. You don't have to do this to prove a point or win my affection. I already love you. You're already everything to me. Go. Do what you love."

Von's smile grew. "I'm not trying to prove a point, Justin. There's nothing to discuss or think about. I don't want it. When I retired, I didn't do so lightly. I wanted to come back home to you. Being here with you—this is my biggest dream coming true. Don't take it from me."

The front door reopened and Luka reappeared. "Sorry to burst back in," he said as he came to stand over them. "Brady and I were discussing matters outside, and I've decided to temporarily withdraw my offer. It's not that I don't want you on my team," Luka rushed to reassure Von. "But there's nothing more important than the people we love. I gave up a lot of responsibility for the team when I married Brady because he takes precedence. I cannot, in good conscience, ask you to take on an end-of-the year race toward the championship when your man needs you here." He handed Von a card. "I know you have my info, but this is Brady's too, so there's no chance you can't get in touch with me should you change your mind about joining us next season." He dipped his chin in Justin's direction. "It was nice meeting you, Justin. I hope you win your fight soon."

"Thank you," Justin said, since he was too shocked to think of anything else.

"Thanks," Von said, setting the card on the end table. "I'm sorry you came all this way for nothing."

Luka smiled, making Justin's stomach churn with jealousy as he realized exactly what Von had seen in the man. His glasses did nothing to hide his gorgeous green eyes, but that smile; it was sexy and sweet. "I never do anything for nothing. It was good seeing you again." He switched his attention Justin's way. "Thank you for allowing us to invade your home. Von is a lucky man."

Heat rushed to Justin's cheeks. He had no idea why he was blushing. All Justin could think was it must've been Luka's power and money bleeding from his pores, making Justin feel overwhelmed and flattered.

"Good evening to you both," Luka said as he headed for the door, seeing himself out.

"You should go after him," Justin said the instant the door closed behind Luka. "If you ask, I'm sure his offer will still stand. You should be on the ice."

To Justin's surprise, Von chuckled. It was a low sound

that curled around his heart and squeezed. Justin couldn't look away from Von's sexy smile. "It amazes me you still think I'm making some huge sacrifice to be with you. This, right here with you, is the only life I want. Leaving here would be the sacrifice, and for what? More money? I don't need that. All I need is right here in this apartment."

Even though Von's claims caused Justin's heart to beat a little faster—in a good way—Justin tried one last argument. "But you're so sexy on the ice."

Von sprang, ripping the blanket from Justin's body before settling on top of him. They were nose to nose and Justin couldn't look anywhere but at Von's sexy blue eyes. They flashed with lust, fire, and love. "I bet I'm even sexier between your thighs," Von said, practically growling each word. After going up on his knees, Von reached over his head and pulled his shirt off, baring his delicious hard chest. He popped the button on his jeans, drawing Justin's gaze to the trail of hair that disappeared inside his jeans. Justin's mouth went dry. His palms itched with the need to rip open Von's jeans and play with the body that belonged to him. That thought gave Justin pause. Von did belong to him. He couldn't deny it any longer. Von wasn't finished making his point, and Justin was happy to let him undress to prove himself. "Are you telling me you'd rather watch me on TV than have me right here?" Von asked, taking Justin's hand and flattening it against his chest. Von's eyes fell closed, as if Justin had been the one to reach out and touch him, and the pleasure was too much.

Von's expression broke Justin. He couldn't hide the way he felt with Von being so real. "If you're asking me if I'd rather rip out my heart than see you unhappy, then yes. Haven't you figured that out yet in the years I've been right here? I've watched you go with a smile on my face, because you had a smile on yours. If you're asking if I'd do it again—yes, I would. I'd do anything for you, because I love you."

The way Von watched him with such intensity should've warned Justin. Nothing could've prepared him for Von's next words. "If you'd do anything to make me smile, then marry me. That's the one dream I have that hasn't come true."

Justin couldn't speak. He could barely breathe. The vulnerability written on Von's face let Justin know he meant it. Von wanted to marry him. This wasn't him trying to make things right. Things were already right. Justin had forgiven Von a long time ago. Not because of some grand gesture that blew Justin away. He'd earned Justin's forgiveness with a steady hand that wiped the past clean.

Von's expression shifted in the face of Justin's silence, as if he braced himself to get shut down. "I guess I screwed you out of a good story—one where I got down on one knee and had a ring."

"No," Justin choked out past his swollen throat.

Pain flashed in Von's eyes. "I get that. It's not like I've done anything to make you want to keep me."

Justin shook his head. "I mean no, you didn't screw me out of those things. Yes, I'll marry you."

Von's expression went blank. He blinked as if Justin's words were slow to sink in. A chuckle escaped Justin as a burst of excitement hit him. The sound seemed to jar something loose inside Von's head. A smile stretched his lips. "You said yes."

Justin nodded. "I did."

Von covered Justin's body with his once more. "Oh my god. I get to keep you."

Justin snorted as Von pressed kisses along his jaw. "You've always had me. Never once have I locked my door against you, even when I've slammed it in your face. All you've ever had to do was turn the knob to find me waiting on the other side." Von met Justin's gaze. The confessions kept coming. "I've just been angry and hurt, but I've never stopped loving you. I could never stop loving you."

"I'm sorry I haven't had the words to make it better. Thank you for hearing them anyhow. I'll make you a proud husband. No one will love you better." Von touched his lips to Justin's, as if sealing his vow with a kiss. "I really want to make love to you," Von whispered against the corner of Justin's mouth. "But I know you don't feel good."

Justin hands slipped down Von's body. "I never feel too bad for you," he said as he shoved his hands inside Von's loosened jeans.

Von sat back on his heels and set his erection free. "I've got a plan," he said, wearing the sweetest smile Justin had ever seen. Justin's body lit with need at the sight. There'd never been another smile he'd ever seen that screamed he was about to get fucked the way Von's did. Von snagged the blanket from the floor and covered them both as he lowered himself onto Justin's body. Working magic with his fingers, he released Justin's throbbing cock. Their dicks brushed, stealing a gasp from Justin. With his weight braced on one elbow and his hand wrapped around both their erections, Von stroked. Justin's hips left the couch.

Von shushed him. "Be still, baby. I've got you. You don't have to do anything but enjoy."

Jesus, he loved this man. Justin couldn't tear his eyes away from the way Von's face mimicked Justin's every emotion. It was hard to hold still as Von worked his cock, but he knew if he moved too much, he'd regret it later. But damn, Von rocked his world. Tiny shivers ran through Justin's body. With every pull of skin on skin, Von brought him closer to the edge. A flush pinkened Von's cheeks. His lips parted slightly and his eyes were unfocused. He was the picture of lust.

Twisted images rose in Justin's mind. He couldn't stop them from falling from his lips. "Goddamn, Von. I want to do everything to you right now. I want to suck your dick and play between your knees. When you give in and let me shove my fingers inside your ass, you have no clue how sexy you look in those moments. You're mush and surrender. Sometimes I think you'd let me do anything if I have you turned on." Von twisted, tearing a moan from Justin. He knew he was pushing Von too far, making him fear he'd come before Justin. Justin wanted it. "Damn, I wish I had your knees shoved high and my tongue in your ass. The way you squirm beneath me is so fucking hot." Von's grip tightened. His movements quickened. Justin saw stars. Sweat broke out on Justin's skin, mixing with Von's. Pressure beat at the head of his cock. "When your salty thick cum covers my tongue—fuck," Justin cried as Von exploded. Hot cum hit the over-sensitized nerve endings in Justin's crown, stealing his orgasm without warning. He gasped and strained, trying desperately to cling to every last sensation before it disappeared.

Von, being perfect, kissed Justin's neck instead of his mouth, because he knew Justin had trouble catching breath after they made love. Each brush of the man's tongue against his throat had Justin panting.

"I love you," Von gasped against Justin's skin. "We'll have a beautiful life," he promised, making the glow of Justin's orgasm seem dim in comparison to their future.

"I know we will," Justin agreed, because it was Von. If anyone would give him their all and never let him down, it was the man in his arms.

EPILOGUE

"*A*re you sure you want to do this?"

Von scoffed at Jamie's question. It was just a baby. He might be a little rough and tumble at times, but he trusted he was intelligent enough to hold a baby without crushing it. "I'm sure I can figure it out."

Jamie eyed Von before switching his gaze to Luna. She smiled. Von couldn't look away. Jamie sighed. "Don't say I didn't warn you," he said, passing Luna over. "Once you hold her, you'll want one."

"Don't be ridiculous," Von said, settling Luna against his chest. Jesus, she had dimples. It was the smallest warmth huddled against him—innocent and in need of protection from the world. Her tiny heart beat against him. The barest puffs of breath brushed his collarbone. Von couldn't stop staring at her. She was amazing. Before he could stop himself, Von worked her tiny fist open so he could inspect her minuscule hands. He'd never been more amazed.

Hawke chuckled. "You called it, baby."

"Yep," Jamie said, sounding entirely too proud of himself.

"Called what?" Justin asked, appearing from the kitchen with drinks in hand for their guests.

"You have to hold this baby," Von said before Jamie could open his mouth again and ruin the moment. The instant Justin settled in beside him, Von passed Luna over—not because he wanted to give her up, but he needed to see the love of his life holding a baby.

"Awww," Justin cooed as he cuddled Luna. Von watched as Justin brushed his jaw on Luna's hair. "She's so soft." Von's throat tightened at the sight. Justin was meant to have a baby in his arms.

"Von wants one," Jamie said as if he couldn't contain it a second longer.

Justin's gaze shot to Von's. He winked, leaving Von wondering what the hell that meant.

"How are you feeling, by the way?" Hawke asked, interrupting their moment.

Justin flashed Hawke a smile. "I'm good. The chemo did its job. I'm in remission and my hair is slowly growing back," Justin said, pointing at his head. "All is good."

"I see all is good here too," Jamie said, motioning between Justin and him.

Justin shifted Luna higher, freeing his left hand. He flashed his wedding ring. "Very good. Thanks."

Jamie huffed, pulling off a damned good injured teenage girl look. "You got married and didn't call me. I thought I was your bestie. I thought, when you got married, we'd braid each other's hair, and I'd catch the bouquet."

Justin's laugh made putting up with Jamie's obnoxiousness worthwhile. "I don't have enough hair to braid and you're already married."

Jamie's shoulders fell, and he toed the carpet like a two

year old. "I know, but I could've gone all diva and made sure you had the bestest wedding of all time."

Justin leaned back and openly smelled Luna's neck. "I had the bestest wedding of all time because Von was there." He sniffed Luna again. "Okay, I really need one of these. She's so sweet."

A smile exploded across Von's face. Jamie might've missed out on giving Justin the bestest wedding ever, but Von would make sure Justin had the bestest life of all time. They were meant to be. He'd never doubted it for a second. Justin had been wrong. They did have what Jamie and Hawke did. They were loyal to each other above all others. They were happy and always would be.

THE END

Author Note: At this point in time, I'm unsure if there will be any more Hard Hit books. I still have ideas, but we'll see. Thank you for reading. If you enjoyed this story, please consider leaving a review.

Additionally, if you're interested in reading Hawke and Jamie's story, their book is called Heart's Strum. You can find it here:

http://mybook.to/UglyEternity3

ABOUT THE AUTHOR

Charity Parkerson is an award winning and multi-published author with several companies. Born with no filter from her brain to her mouth, she decided to take this odd quirk and insert it in her characters.

*2015 Readers' Favorite Award Winner
  *Winner of 2, 2014 Readers' Favorite Awards
  *2015 Passionate Plume Award Finalist
  *2013 Readers' Favorite Award Winner
  *2013 Reviewers' Choice Award Winner
  *2012 ARRA Finalist for Favorite Paranormal Romance
  *Five time winner of The Mistress of the Darkpath

Connect with her online:

--Join my street team: facebook.com/TeamCharityParkerson
  --Sign up for my newsletter: http://bit.ly/CharityNews
  --Website: charityparkerson.com
  --Facebook: facebook.com/authorCharityParkerson
  facebook.com/TheMenofSin
  --Twitter: twitter.com/CharityParkerso

http://www.charityparkerson.com/hard-hit

www.charityparkerson.com
admin@charityparkerson.com